Eerie Charms of the Short Story

Fantasy, Mystery, & Horror

Eerie Charms
of the Short Story
Fantasy, Mystery, & Horror

Patricia A. Guthrie

Fresh Ink Group

Guntersville

Eerie Charms of the Short Story:
Fantasy, Mystery, and Horror

Copyright © 2018-2022
by Patricia A. Guthrie
All rights reserved

Fresh Ink Group
An Imprint of:
The Fresh Ink Group, LLC
1021 Blount Avenue #931
Guntersville, AL 35976
Email: info@FreshInkGroup.com
FreshInkGroup.com

Edition 1.0   2022

Cover design by Stephen Geez / FIG
Mirror-reflection art by Anik / FIG
Book design by Amit Dey / FIG
Associate publisher Lauren A. Smith / FIG

"Razz Upon the Sheep" appeared in *The Cassette*, Spring 2001

Cataloging-in-Publication Recommendations:
FIC029000   FICTION / Short Stories (single author)
FIC009040   FICTION / Fantasy / Collections & Anthologies
FIC030000   FICTION / Thrillers / Suspense

Library of Congress Control Number: 2022915957

ISBN-13: 978-1-947893-38-2 Papercover
ISBN-13: 978-1-947893-39-9 Hardcover
ISBN-13: 978-1-947893-44-3 Ebooks

Acknowledgements

v

*Dedicated to short-story writers everywhere.
I know how hard you work and how hard short stories
and flash fiction are to create.*

*To all my readers and reviewers: You are my angels.
I hope you enjoy these eerie tales.*

Table of Contents

Sarpati

*A snake decides the fate of the world.
A spoof on the Adam and Eve story told from the snake's
point-of-view. Sarpati means "snake" in Greek.*

"So, Sarpati. What do you have for me today?" Lucifer sat with his back against a highly polished rosewood desk with his clawed feet on a credenza, gazing out the window. He didn't bother to look at his growing staff. He was more interested in the newest species of dockworkers hauling cargo from passing freighters. Some evolved from the Neanderthal pedigrees. They were a colorful variety, using the smaller versions of brontosaurs who'd managed to survive the ice-age disaster to haul cargo for them. And some who'd just appeared one day in a practical application: small and wiry for speed, large head capacity for brainpower, and eyes as large as saucers for better night vision.

He was interested in all of God's creatures. Some had already joined his organization; others were still working for the enemy. He had to figure a way to win them over. He glanced at the piers on the Pishone River that fed into the Gulf and beyond to the heavens.

"Hey, Luce . . . er, Mr. Lucifer, Sir. How do you like your new office?" the snake asked, looking and hissing approval at his boss's new digs.

"Well, it ain't paradise, but it's home. It's nice being an entrepreneur. No one can tell me what to do anymore." He yelled through the open French-style windows and into the clouds. "Did you hear that?"

A distant blast of thunder seemed to answer his question.

In reply, Mr. Lucifer snatched his nameplate—which read, Mephistopheles S. Lucifer, President Local 666—and threw it out the window. It boomeranged from a sudden wind surge and crashed back down on his desk, scattering a stack of union applications.

"Damn," he said. "Just because I tried to organize his obstinate angels for him, he fires me. Throws me out like yesterday's news." His booming voice knocked Sarpati onto the floor. "Fine way to treat a dedicated employee."

For the short time Sarpati had been in the employ of God's one and only fallen angel, the constant bantering back and forth never ceased to amaze him. It provided him, who'd never been in the good graces of the man upstairs anyhow, with constant entertainment. Here, he had an opportunity for success beyond his wildest imagination, and he wasn't about to let it slip through his fingers. So, he would cheer on his employer with a "Go get him, Mr. Luce" and a "Right on, boss." Then, they'd sip on some elderberry wine and smoke cigars. This time, however, was different.

Lucifer slowly turned in his swivel chair with a sardonic smile and said, "Got a job for you."

The serpent crawled back onto his chair and faced the gaunt mask with high cheekbones and dark, pooled eyes. Sarpati's tongue slid in and out as he leered, eyes narrowing down to tiny slits. "What's the job, boss?" His tiny front legs rubbed against each other, and his lean, long green body squirmed in anticipation.

"You know the new couple in Eden?"

"You mean the ones with two legs? The ones called *humans*?"

"Yessss."

"The ones with more hair on their heads than on the rest of 'em?"

"Grrrr-yessss."

Sarpati liked to play, and he hardly noticed the waning patience of Lucifer.

"What? Adam and Eve?" He was on a roll.

Lucifer cut through him like a knife slicing a piece of choice Grade-A meat. "I *want* them."

"Hey, man. I don't know," Sarpati whined. "The Head Honcho made them. They're pretty happy where they are."

"The who?" Lucifer glared. "The head *who*?" A smoked-filled flame blew from his nostrils, threatened to burn the snake to a wrinkled crisp.

Sarpati hadn't anticipated the wrath of Hell on his head. His rubbery textured skin felt prickly like it did when one of those dumb angels was close. He had a bad feeling about interfering with God's newest creations. Still, he felt a more immediate threat—even a foreboding—if he crossed his boss.

"All the better. I want you . . ." Lucifer said, losing all pretense of composure, "to get them for me." He grabbed Sarpati by his long winding neck and threatened to throttle him.

"How?" The snake hissed, trying to catch his breath.

"That, my dear employee, is up to you. You have exactly two days."

Lucifer picked up Sarpati by his tail with a demonic roar and hurled him out of his office. He bounced off the wall and onto the floor, gathered himself together, and scurried as quickly as he could down the stairs and onto the wharf. The snake rested by the river, nursing his wounds and shedding some skin, waiting to catch a passing freighter on its way to Eden. As he basked in the beautiful sun created by his employer's main business rival, he saw giant tentacles forming from Lucifer's head. They reached out from the third-story window into the sky, momentarily blocking the solar warmth. The demonic roar set Sarpati about his task, but he wondered just what his boss was up to now.

Continuing to sun himself, he looked over the water at the approaching vessel. *So, Sarpi,* he thought, pleased with the nickname he'd coined for himself, *how do I get them to work for the Boss? They have a beautiful garden, plenty of food, and shelter. What don't they have?* He scratched a particularly itchy spot on his back by rolling over and sliding up and down as he continued pondering the question.

The freighter pulled alongside the dock, and cargos of supplies appeared as if by magic.

"Sending more trees out to Eden Island," one of God's crewmen said. He had a broad head, pin-pointy eye, wide nostrils, and an I'd-rather-be-drinking attitude.

"What's the route?" his mate asked, anxious to get the details out of the way, so he could join his supervisor for a beer.

His superior scowled. "Down the Pishone River past Havilah. Then, we catch the Gihon up to the Tigress and reach Eden in three hours."

"What's on Eden?"

"A garden paradise for a new species called *humans* the boss just created. We're delivering a special variety of apple trees that God's using as a learning tool for these new creatures. It's still in the experimental stage, so hands *off*. We don't touch the tree. Orders."

"Experimental, eh?" His mate asked, "What does this one do?" He pointed to a tree being hauled on the deck.

"Oh, that's the Tree of Mathematics."

"Math . . . e, *what?*" He shook his furry face and shrugged bony shoulders that connected arms nearly the length of his entire body.

"Don't ask me. I don't know. I just know we don't touch the apple trees."

"Okay, okay. They're probably wormy apples anyway," the other man replied.

"Yeah, yeah," his supervisor said. "Maybe on the way back, we can stop in Havilah. You'll love the city. Paved with gold. We can catch the *Neanderthal Ladies* act at the Midas Touch Cabaret." Their voices drifted off as they dragged the trees down into the cargo hold.

Sarpati picked up his scaly head and suddenly knew what he had to do. Aha . . . that's the key. Knowledge . . . the tree. I'll bet they'll want to know stuff. With that, Sarpati slithered into a crate of oranges and, feeling smug, coiled himself up into a ball and took a nap. He didn't even wake up when the container was carried onto the ship.

While supplies were being unloaded onto the docks in Eden, four hours later, Sarpati made his own exit from the freighter.

There were trees of all varieties scattered throughout Paradise Gardens, but the fruit trees were the most outstanding. One stood apart from all the rest; its apples, big, red, and luscious looking, hanging off its branches like trophies of achievement. It was the cornerstone of the garden—the granddaddy of them all.

Each apple was labeled with a skill; *Literature by up-and-coming authors of the next few centuries, Writing techniques throughout the coming ages, Religious doctrines of the future,* and *Good and evil — now and always.* And it was under this tree which offered its cool shade from the brilliant but hot sunshine, where Sarpati found the woman resting, eating a piece of fruit.

Sarpati utilized his small reptilian legs to crawl through the luxurious blades of grass, feeling cool dampness on his skin. This wasn't such a bad assignment, after all. He couldn't think of another job that would provide him with the time and means to travel. He wondered if the woman had ever seen a snake before. He assumed she didn't know anything about anything.

The two-legged creature named Eve was different than any creature he'd ever seen. Her skin was not as hard or callous, nor flaky as his, but smoother. Unlike his brownish-gray color, hers was more a light beige hue. And, although her hair didn't grow over her body like the other creatures, it flowed from her head, coming down in waves of a flaxen gold color. It hung longer than any he'd ever seen, covering her entire body with its silky texture. He wondered if so much hair coming from so little space might be uncomfortable.

Unusual, he thought—definitely different. He decided to use the direct approach.

"Thought you weren't supposed to eat from any of the trees," he said.

"Oh . . ." The woman looked startled. Her eyes darted around, first up at the trees, then down at the ground, until they finally arrived on the snake hiding in the grass. "Who are you?" she asked.

"Sarpati's the name, and fruit tree's my game. Please to meet you," he replied, entwining himself around the woman's right leg and peering up into her face.

"*What* are you?" she asked again. "I've never seen anything quite like you before."

"Madam, I . . . ," he said, levitating, so his head stood flat and parallel to her face, ". . . am a snake," he finished proudly. "And you?" He was curious.

"I am a human," she said. "And I'm waiting for my husband to come back."

"Your what?"

"Husband. His name is Adam, and I'm Eve."

"What strange names," Sarpati said, trying to keep the conversation going.

"Yes, God made us last week. We're here to live a good life. We are supposed to keep out of trouble, and we get to live in this beautiful place where there is an abundance of food to eat. All we have to do is reach out for it." She smiled.

Piece of cake, Sarpati thought. Dumb as a box of rocks.

"We can eat from any of these trees except this one," she said, pointing to the great apple tree above her. "God said that if we ate from it, we'd die."

"Not true," said the serpent, with a wicked gleam in his yellow eyes. "You won't die. You'll learn what God knows. He's used to controlling everything. He couldn't stand it if you knew as much as he does."

"Have you really met God?" Eve asked.

"Sure, met him hundreds of times," the snake lied. "What's more, my boss used to work for him."

"Your boss. Who's he?"

"Not important. He just feels that everyone is entitled to an education."

Sarpati waved his head back and forth in front of her face, mesmerizing her.

She seemed fascinated and didn't move.

"Now," he said. "Does that tree look evil to you?"

Eve sprang back to life, looking up at its towering branches. "No."

"Wouldn't you like to know the difference between good and evil?" he asked, slowly seducing her again with his hypnotic stare.

"Yes," she responded. "Er . . . no." She pulled back, pushing him off her leg with her other foot.

"Do you know how good these apples are?" he asked, challenging her as he crawled up her other leg.

"No."

"Wouldn't you like to?" he questioned.

"I don't think . . ." Her eyes rested on his tiny front foot as it moved back and forth in an even, steady, mesmerizing manner. "Yee . . . es," she said.

Like a flash, he slithered up the tree and shook a large branch until the most beautiful and juiciest specimen fell at her feet.

"Hello, pretty. What do you have there?" The man walked up the path carrying fruit of all varieties. He appeared to be favoring his left side.

"Adam, what's wrong with your side?" Eve asked.

"Just my ribs. They still hurt where he took . . . well, you know." Adam stared at the apple Eve had just picked off the ground.

"Hell . . . o. Let me introduce myself," Sarpati said.

Startled, Adam spun around to face the voice.

"Sarpati's the name, and fruit tree's my game. And, let me say, there isn't a finer fruit in this whole garden than the one your wife is holding."

"Uh . . . we're not supposed to eat those," Adam said with a puzzled expression on his face.

"No? Oh, perhaps you weren't in the beginning."

"Beginning?"

"Yeah. They used to be poison. At least, that was the rhetoric."

"Rhetor . . . who?"

"Nonsense. Nothing but nonsense. My employer realized the error of his ways and asked me to come and tell you that eating from this tree is ju . . . sst fine. In fact, he wants you to." Sarpati laughed to himself as Adam and Eve looked perplexed. He continued, "And, he wants you to know that you can get a first-rate education by just taking one teeny bite."

"An ed . . . u . . . what?" Adam asked.

"Education. Knowledge. You'll get to know stuff. Almost as much as me."

"Well, if he said so," Eve said, fondling the apple and smelling it.

"Eve?" Adam looked doubtful.

"Go on . . . what's the matter?" The snake taunted her. "Afraid?"

"No," Eve said. "I'm not afraid." She stood for a moment as though waiting to see what would happen, then she bit into the apple.

"Good?" The snake crooned, and his tongue slid out of his mouth and circled his lips.

Eve bit down again and handed the apple to her husband. Her voice took on a strange tone.

"Adam . . . eat it."

The snake giggled with glee.

"No . . . Eve . . . I don't think . . ." Adam said.

"Eat it," Eve commanded.

Adam obeyed.

Sarpati rested on the grass and watched the two interact. Their eyes growing wide with astonishment and wonder at the world around them.

Suddenly, from somewhere out of the east, a loud booming laugh charged over the land. "They're mine," it said, repeating over and over.

Without losing a beat, another sound, louder and more compelling, was heard coming from the sky, shattering the complacent garden. Adam and Eve ran for cover. Sarpati hid in the tree.

"Adam! Eve!" The voice became louder and more focused and seemed to swirl into a physical manifestation—a presence.

Two small, cowering voices whimpered from behind a clump of trees. "Uh-oh."

God's presence materialized in the form of a very large and muscular human, more intimidating than Lucifer, even on his worst days. Sarpati began to think that maybe he'd formed the wrong alliance.

"All right, you two . . . . Out," God demanded.

Adam and Eve surfaced, wearing an attempt at aprons strung together by fig leaves.

Even Sarpati raised an eyebrow and tried not to snicker.

God was not amused. "What's that?"

"Uh . . ." Adam said, trying to formulate his newly acquired thoughts.

"We're naked," Eve said. "We're not supposed to be."

"What the . . . ?" God responded. Then he saw the apple.

"So that's why Lucifer was laughing so hard. You ate the apple. How many times have I told you . . . *don't go near the apple tree?*"

"Uh . . . about forty," Adam said.

"And you did it anyway?" God asked in a tone of total disbelief.

"She made me do it," Adam said.

"Did not."

"Did too."

"Stop that this instant," God said. "Who did it first?"

"She did."

"Did you?"

"Er . . . he made me do it," Eve replied, pouting and pointing to Sarpati who was hanging on a tree limb waiting to see who would come out on top.

"You . . . a snake?"

God finally focused on Sarpati and, without touching him, sent him crashing to the ground.

"Ou . . . ch."

"Of all the ungrateful children, this takes the cake. I work my fingers to the bone, trying to provide a nice, easy life for you . . . no worry, no cares, and this is how you repay me?"

God paused and paced for several moments. "Okay. So, it's going to be like this. You don't seem to have any respect for authority, so you'll have to work for a living just like all the rest of us.

"And you, Eve, you want knowledge? Well, you've got it. You're going to learn just how hard it is to be a parent. You're going to have ungrateful kids and raise them all by yourselves.

"Adam. You're going to have to provide for these ungrateful brats. See how you like it. And, if it doesn't work out, don't come crying to me."

God stopped his tirade just long enough to glance at Sarpati, who had hidden behind the tree.

"You . . . you slithering piece of slimy deceit . . . you're not off the hook either. You're not going to tread all over my creatures again. Do you hear?" God pointed one massive finger, and an electrical current swept through the air aimed directly at the unfortunate serpent. "No longer will you be able to walk like everyone else. Now you'll see how it feels to be trampled . . . stomped on . . . kicked around."

The reptilian legs seemed to just disappear—vanished into thin air. Sarpati, clinging to the tree, suddenly fell off, bounced onto the ground, and landed just behind Eve's feet.

Startled, she jumped back, landing firmly on what once had been his tail.

"Ouch, watch that," he shouted. No one heard. His voice had disappeared along with his legs. As he slithered out of sight and out of his trusted position as Lucifer's first assistant, he heard God giving his offspring final instructions.

"Okay, back to your education. Eve, you're going to learn to cook and clean and make clothes. Adam, I'm giving you a nice choice piece of desert land to settle on and learn how to manage. With a little work, maybe in . . . oh, say three . . . four hundred years and some yet to be invented technology, you can make something out of it."

Back where the River Pishone meets the Gulf, Mephistopheles S. Lucifer, President of Local 666, met with his newest applicant applying for the recently opened position of top henchman.

The Slot Machine

A slot machine decides who wins and who loses.

Once a bright, shiny, gorgeous machine lived in a luxurious casino, now its lights have gone out, and sadness reigns in the machine room. But I'll let you read Midas's story for yourself.

"Welcome to my house. I'm a slot machine, and my name is Midas. I'm not just an ordinary slot machine, mind you, but high-class with bells and whistles. I whirl, ding, and play tunes. Why the games on me alone would make the most avid slot player tingle with anticipation.

"If you've never been to my place, let me give you a brief tour. When you enter my vast room, bright, glittering lights and bells assault your senses. You see rows and rows of my brothers and sisters, all lined up, one after another. Some distant cousins take the big bucks, but we don't generally speak. They like to think they're better than we are, but of course, they're wrong. I've heard tales of smaller, neighboring rooms that have big tables where they play for really high stakes, but I've never seen them in person, so I can only guess.

"Attached to the ceiling are constant lights that flicker on and off, like little stars. Colorful disco lights flash, and the air has a pungent smell of smoke and sweat all the time. I never know whether it's day or night because there are no windows. The patrons don't need to know the time because they're too busy being lulled by the constant dings of the winning machines. Ooh, that does my heart good. I'm not a mean machine, you know.

"You can win with me.

"I must admit, I have my favorites. I've become quite attached to a young lady named Maureen Goldstein. Now, I consider myself a very fair slot machine, but when she comes by, if there's anyone else playing, I immediately tighten up, and they start to lose. Disgusted, they usually move on, leaving her free to play me.

"Maureen Goldstein. I know her name because she told me. She's told me many other things. I've learned all about her being a widow left alone with three small children. Machines aren't supposed to have feelings but give me a break. I'm not entirely heartless. Nor am I indifferent to the other souls who come to play. You'd be surprised at the stories I hear. Some tell me their whole life history. Some just put their money in, touch the card pictures and stare, blankly. One guy even tried to beat me up. The guards took care of that.

"Maureen was the only one who actually gave me a name. She calls me *Midas* in her kind, sweet voice, and it's enough to loosen my inner-workings—loose enough to give her a great poker hand.

"This afternoon, the bosses came 'round and tightened me—really hard. The constant crowd flow came and went. Most were disappointed in their efforts and moved on to seek their fortunes at other machines.

"Maureen came along just as this guy, sitting in my seat, got up and moved. She sat down, and suddenly, my screws came loose. I felt them pop and whir."

"Hello, Midas," she said.

"Meanwhile, the workers shook me again and shook their heads."

"No idea what's wrong with this machine," they said, before moving to another machine.

"I tried to purr out my usual greeting, and when she slid her twenty-dollar bill into my slot—she *always* brought a twenty—I went berserk. She could do no wrong. Her hands played me like a finely tuned fiddle. That felt good! She tickled my lever, and I dealt her a four-of-a-kind. Bingo. Two-hundred-credits. Next, I gave her a full house and another one hundred fifty credits.

"Maureen screamed in delight. A three of a kind and pairs soon followed. Maureen jumped up and down on my seat. As she placed her bet, her gentle touch on my faceplate was more than I could bear.

"Now, she played Double-Up. I mentally nudged her mind toward the correct cards, and each time she won. I pulled out all the stops. Whistles blew, sirens wailed, lights flashed, and a version of the *Hallelujah Chorus* played from of my machine. Everyone was standing and applauding Maureen's good fortune. Tokens gushed out of my innards. An attendant appeared, followed closely by two security guards."

"Congratulations, young lady," he said.

"All good things must come to an end. With one last pat, she said, "Oh, Midas, you've just paid off my mortgage. Thank you."

"I could have told her that just her caresses were enough, thanks. I dreaded her leaving.

"I had a good reason. Two men with watchful eyes and perpetual frowns hovered in the area, watching the proceedings. They sauntered over, pulled some levers, took off my back, pulled some wires, and slammed me a couple of times. They shook their heads. This wasn't funny. It hurt!

"Later came the ultimate humiliation. Some men with the word *Maintenance* written on their spanking white polo shirts came and hauled me away that night. They removed my back, took apart my faceplate, and worst of all, they pulled off my magnificent top—my crowning glory—to my everlasting shame. They shook their heads and gave me one last kick for good measure. Then they left me torn apart, some of me scattered all over the maintenance room, some even adorning the tops of other sad-looking machines.

"Oh, dear. It seems like months since the door last opened. I stand now, lonely and forlorn, in the repair shop, waiting to get *fixed*."

"And so ends the sad tale of Midas, my favorite slot machine. Today I saw the reject trucks pull up to the casino's back door and haul him away. His parts will be picked off his frame and, probably, screwed into another up-and-coming and unsuspecting slot machine. I'm the woman whose life Midas saved. My life is now happy with money, a new husband (a slot machine repairman), and a new house."

"Still, part of me is sad."

Broken Toys in the Attic

Abused and neglected toys get revenge.

"Ma . . . mm . . . ee." Melissa Anne Greenwood belonged to the voice that blasted throughout the house sounding more like an angry hyena than a little girl of six.

Melissa sat in the middle of her bed, staring at favorite toys formally displayed on bookcases, rocking chairs, toy boxes, and a corner hutch. She didn't feel like playing with any of them. Old Neddie, the rocking horse, once the pride and joy of the nursery, now had a shattered front leg. Pooh Bear, a well-beloved antique, had one missing glass eye, and of course, Sir Scottie, the stuffed black Scottie dog, had the stuffing torn out and sewn back more times than her mother could count. None of them would do today. They were boring. She bounced off the old-fashioned sleigh bed, defaced from temper tantrums, and walked out of her room toward the stairs.

"Mommy?"

No answer.

Now, her voice demanded, "Ma . . . mm . . . ee."

"Melissa, what is it? I'm busy." Her mother came to the stairs, carrying an infant in her arms and pushing a laundry basket with her foot. Strands of dark hair dangled over her face, while dark circles under her eyes emphasized strain. She looked frazzled.

"Mommy, I'm bored."

"Your toys, Melissa. Play with your toys."

"But, Mommy, I've played with them."

Melissa became more impatient. She wanted to play with her Mommy, but her mother was always preoccupied with the baby. She hated her little brother.

"Mommy, why don't you ever play with me anymore?"

"Oh, honey, I can't right now."

"Mommy!" Melissa screamed. She pitched herself forward onto the landing and threw one of the world's greatest temper tantrums.

"Melissa Anne Greenwood, if you don't stop that this instant, I will really give you something to scream about." Stepping around the plastic basket and readjusting the baby, she took two steps up the stairs. Even through the thick carpet, her feet made an adequate stomp.

Melissa decided she'd probably better stop—knowing her mother meant it this time.

"Okay, Mommy." She forced sobs that didn't quite work and then manipulated her voice almost down to a whisper. "I'm finished now."

"Good. Now go find something to play with . . . and don't go near the attic."

"Okay, Mommy."

Melissa went back into her room and, flinging Pooh Bear on the floor, plunked herself down on Pooh's small rocking chair. The chair was too small and cracked under her weight. She slipped on the floor.

She looked at her many games, books, toys, and stuffed animals, all her friends until recently. After all, they had always talked to her. They shared secrets about what Mommy did when she came up to her room to clean—the things she looked at and the things she looked behind. Melissa had learned to write certain words, like *I luv u mommy*, and put them where she thought her mommy would look. It worked perfectly. She got hugs and new toys.

And the old toys? She'd discarded her old friends when the new ones arrived and relegated them to the attic—yesterday's news. Lately, however, even her new toys bored her—ever since that baby came.

Before her brother was born, Old Ned had as strong a front leg as had ever been carved. Pooh Bear was brand new, straight from Toys 'R' Us, and Old Scottie—well, Old Scottie had been her mother's favorite toy from childhood. All were victims of Melissa's displeasure. She delighted in every tear shed each time Mommy had to sew Old Scottie back together.

Melissa felt hateful.

"Now, it's your turn." A vicious grin replaced the pout. "Next week, I'll have my daddy put you in the attic, too. I'll get new toys. Toys better 'n you. *Way* better. Maybe, I'll even throw you in the garbage." She looked at each toy with contempt, turned on her heels, and started to leave her betrayed favorites.

Suddenly, something in the corner of her eye caught her attention, and she spun around. She couldn't be sure. Did Old Ned actually seem to rock a little—back and forth, back and forth? Was Old Scottie attempting to make a sound that said, "No?" And did Pooh Bear's one good eye appear to widen, just a little?

As soon as she turned, all stuffed animal activity ceased. No, she decided, it was only her imagination.

The forbidden attic was the only room that still intrigued Melissa, the only place not explored. It was the place where they put things they no longer wanted. It was where Mommy's stuff was and where they put Nanny's things when she went away. Of course, she knew Nanny hadn't really gone anywhere. She'd just died.

A set of steep, wooden stairs led from the end of the hall to the attic. Melissa climbed cautiously, careful not to make any creaking noises her mother might hear. The door stood on a small landing at the head of the stairs. Small but determined fingers and arms tugged at a knob that wouldn't give. Locked. She jerked again and succeed in hurting her arm.

Frustrated, she was about ready to turn and go back downstairs when she spotted a silver key on an antique gold ring hanging to the right of the door. It was just beyond her reach. She stood on her tiptoes—no luck. She leaped into the air and landed on her rear, crinkling the back of her blue and white play dress.

"Ouch!" She nearly cried but decided to get back up instead. She brushed herself off and started all over again.

One, two, three leaps later, Melissa jingled the key hard enough so that the object of her frustration flipped off the hook and landed on the floor. She punished the recalcitrant key by viciously thrusting it into the keyhole. Then, smug with the self-satisfaction of a thief who'd broken into an uncrackable safe, she turned the key and finally the knob. She was in.

As soon as she entered, Melissa noticed the darkness. At the far end of the room, a lone triangular stained-glass window had become so dirty throughout the years, only a glimmer of outside light could pass through its windowpane. A light bulb hung from the ceiling, but the string was too short for her to reach, and the only other available light poured in through the open door behind her.

Picture frames, suitcases, furniture pieces, and a bunch of boxes containing many musty books filled the room. A wooden rocking chair held all varieties of stuffed animals, some of which Melissa recognized as playmates from her baby days. She set out to investigate every nook and cranny. First, she crunched old clothes, broke some figurines, squeezed baby dolls, a stuffed gorilla, and fiddled with an old play cash register and toy soldiers from her father's day.

Melissa was so absorbed in the objects that she backed into a figure dressed in a long black dress with a mink stole. It wore a wide brim hat and had a triple strand of pearls irregularly wound around its neck. The face was a pasty sort of chalk color with cheeks that might have come from a crayon box and lips that were a deep cherry red. A cavernous hole for a mouth showed marked protruding teeth locked in a welcoming yet ghastly smile. She gaped in horror at the apparition of what appeared to be—Granny.

Suddenly, the light was gone.

The attic door had swung shut with such force it knocked something over, which crashed into her. She screamed. She tried to adjust her eyes, but it was pitch black, except for tiny pinpricks of red and green lights emanating from the stained glass. A macabre sense of movement coming from all directions seemed to twirl around her, moving faster and faster until she felt dizzy and disoriented. She felt a cold stream of air blast through her, and something wound around her arm, holding her fast.

She screamed with all her might. "Mommy!" Her voice seemed to resound throughout the room. "Mommy!" she cried out again. Then, the other voices started to join in, one right after the other.

They started as a whisper, "Melissa . . . Oh, Melissa . . . we know you're here, Melissa."

"We know. We know!"

"You don't love us anymore, Melissa."

"Who are you?" She choked out the words--just barely.

Then, another voice called—cajoling, beckoning. "Melissa, dear Melissa."

It couldn't be. Could it? Nanny was dead!

"Nanny?" Melissa murmured, taking in shallow gasps of air. No! Nanny was dead. She'd watched her fall down the stairs. After she'd pushed her.

"Did you come to play with Nanny?"

"Nan . . . Na . . . na . . . na . . . Nanny . . ." The voices chimed in as a chorus.

"Did you come to play with Nanny?" the first voice bellowed.

Struggling to break free, she felt her restraint shatter into a thousand tiny fragments, which attacked her from all sides. Terrified, she tried to escape but tripped over something and fell to her knees. It's all my toys, she thought, coming to get me.

Getting up in a blind panic, she tried to run again, but fingers grabbed her from behind, catching her like a rabbit in a snare.

Now, voices came from every side. They seemed to originate from forgotten toys and forgotten relatives, their memories trapped in the attic—no differently than her.

Melissa screamed in terror, and they laughed in response.

"You'll never get out of here," one said.

"This is where they dump you when they don't want you anymore," another said.

"Like us. Like us. Like us." Voices echoed. They came from the ceiling, from her grandmother, from the toys, from the . . .

"You don't want us anymore, Melissa, but we want you."

Melissa let out another shriek. "Mommy!" She suddenly felt sorry for every bad thing she'd ever done.

"They don't want you anymore; they don't want bad little girls," another voice said.

"Melissa . . . Melissa." The voices started chanting—fingers reaching to stroke her face and her arms. "Melissa . . . Melissa . . ."

She struggled to break free, screaming and fighting, as they also struggled to reach her—laughing, mimicking, and taunting. "Mommy . . . Mommy . . . Mommy."

The whirlwind of apparitional activity escalated. The penetrating cold in the room created frigid chills of pain, and a rush of air blinded her to such an extent she had to keep her eyes closed tight. She thought she felt the clammy fingers of old dolls and the furry paws of stuffed animals choking her. Nanny's ever-present voice uttered, "Let's play . . . Let's play," followed by an eerie cackle.

"We want to play," the voice that sounded like Nanny uttered. "We want to play with the baby, Melissa. Bring us the baby."

"Nanny?" She shook all over—from the cold and from her fear.

When Melissa became convinced that life as she knew it was over, the attic door sprung open, and all activity ceased. She turned in terror and apprehension.

"My God, Melissa . . . Baby. Didn't I tell you never to go into the attic?"

As the light poured in, Melissa saw only the old treasures locked in the attic. Nanny returned to a dressmaker's mannequin, clad in the mink stole and old-fashioned black silk dress. Its high-collared neckline propped up a Styrofoam head adorned with a wig and hat. The pearls, however, were no longer around the neck but scattered over the floor.

There were no apparitions; not one thing appeared sinister.

Melissa felt a tug at her skirt. She jerked her head around and found nothing—nothing but a faint echo repeated over and over. "The baby, Melissa. Don't forget the baby. Bring me the baby . . ."

"Mommy, did you hear that?" Melissa whispered.

"Hear what, baby?" Her mother replied, scooping her into her arms. "Shh. There's nothing here."

Melissa wasn't convinced. As her mother carried her downstairs, Melissa thought she could hear the choral voices of the past, faintly laughing and mimicking.

"Didn't I tell you never to go into the attic? Didn't I tell you never to go into the attic? Didn't I tell . . . ?"

Later that evening, little Melissa Anne Greenwood wondered how she could drag that stupid baby all the way up those stairs.

The Painting

A painting invites an abused housewife into its landscape.

Sheila stared out a tiny, cracked apartment window that overlooked the dark and oppressive streets of Manhattan's lower east side. Routinely, the landlord skimped on the heat, and she buried herself in a blanket. She was so cold—her fingers numb.

She hated her life, hated her husband for bringing her here. He'd promised her Park Avenue and given her lower East Side. He'd promised a loving household filled with children and given her multiple beatings stemming from his own frustrated, alcoholic existence.

A tear-stained painting of her mother's old farmhouse perched precariously on her lap. In his youth, her husband had painted the picture for her birthday—the only thing he'd ever given her that she'd cherished.

She could almost picture herself in the setting. The steps from the screened-in porch met a winding, country road circling around a lake. Almost daily, she'd ridden her horse, Crackers, down this road and into town.

Her ice-cold fingers touched the painting and felt gravel. Strange. She thought she smelled fresh clumps of mowed grass mingling with blueberry pancakes and heard the neighing of horses in the back pasture. Couldn't be.

Mesmerized, she imagined floating clouds hovering high in the sky as she fell into a stupor.

Sheila woke and felt herself swaying from side to side. Disoriented, she imagined the clip-clop of horses' hooves rising from somewhere below and then realized this was not her imagination. The sun's rays warmed her cold cheeks while soft breezes caressed her bruised shoulders, and the silky coat of her old horse healed her spirit. If this were a dream, she prayed she'd never wake from its compelling illusions. Crackers walked close to the shoreline, stepping in occasionally. The water drenched her lower pant legs. Hot above, cool beneath. How long could she stay here? Forever, she hoped. Forever. There was the porch of her parent's farmhouse. A party going on. Her mother cutting a cake, her father grilling steaks. How was that possible? They'd been dead for many years.

So, was she dead too? She certainly hoped so. The people called to her, welcoming her home. Maybe she was dead.

For a long time, her husband searched for his missing wife. The police nearly arrested him for her murder but never found evidence she was even dead.

Then one day, while looking at the painting, he noticed the figure of a woman resembling his wife, riding a horse.

"I'll be damned," he said. "I never noticed that before." He decided he was hallucinating. Drunk again.

Once again, he decided it couldn't be.

The Fair Lady

A Hungarian and malevolent fairy dances men to death.

"The couple's Mercedes broke through the guardrail of the Warren Street Bridge and plunged into the river. One witness claimed he saw a horse running across the road, but the police have found no evidence."

Allison McKinley, the owner of The Fair Lady Bed and Breakfast, clicked off the television. So that's why the Monroe's hadn't checked in. Not only had a couple lost their lives, but The Fair Lady lost another client. She sighed.

Last week, an elderly guest from Hungary passed during the night from a heart attack.

She settled into hanging ornaments onto the seven-foot Christmas tree that centered the bay window. Sadness welled into a lump in her throat.

More negative publicity. So far, none of the guests canceled, but it would only be a matter of time until those ominous calls began with "We've made other plans . . ."

What more could go wrong? Allison shivered. Death comes in threes. She shook off the apprehension and picked an ornament from the box. She stood on a chair and still had to tip the top branch.

The village church bells chimed six as she cleaned up the ornament boxes and turned on the tree lights. The silver tinsel sparkled. The ornaments turned into a colorful kaleidoscope of drummer boys, rocking horses, and candy canes.

Headlights lit up the room as a car pulled into the driveway. Tom, thank God. Christmas brought too many depressed patients to her psychiatrist husband.

The back door slammed, and footsteps stamped into the kitchen.

"Allie, I'm home." Tom McKinley entered the room wearing a somber expression. When he looked around the room, a smile slowly spread across his face. He put his arm around her.

"Sad news about the Monroe's," Tom said. "Second time in a month a guest has died."

Allison let out a hesitant chuckle. "They check into The Fair Lady and never check out."

"Hey, babe. It's going to be all right." He pulled her into him. "We can't get a reputation because of an accident. And Mr. Kalman was elderly. He had a weak heart."

"Yes, but . . ."

"Allie," Tom whispered. "Let's sit." He took her hand and pulled her down beside him on the couch. "The sheriff dropped by my office."

"And?"

"Their car went out of control."

"I'd imagine. Spinning on the ice . . ."

"Honey, there wasn't any ice on the bridge. The plows came through and salted. The sheriff said they looked as though they'd seen something terrible."

Allison shuddered and pulled back from her husband. Something in his tone frightened her. "Like what?"

"Like the expression of the man who'd died upstairs?" Tom's face clouded. "Someone saw a horse running loose before the car went over."

Her mouth dropped open. "A loose horse?"

"Nobody else saw the horse or found hoof prints."

"But—it was snowing. The tracks could have been covered."

"There's more."

"More?"

"Somebody spotted a white horse this afternoon, trotting for our barn."

Allison stood up. "Nonsense. We have no horses in our barn."

"I checked to see if one might have made himself at home, but there wasn't anything. Not even a track."

Allison started to respond when the doorbell rang.

Tom shrugged and got up. "I wish they'd come through the side entrance."

"Oh, I forgot to tell you. This afternoon, a woman called and made a reservation."

A woman stood on the porch dressed in white from her woolen fur-lined coat to knee-high boots. Her pale face might have blended into the neckline if it hadn't been for the black hair that flowed down her shoulders.

Allison made one quick analysis. Ethereal. Allison's glance at Tom wasn't entirely voluntary.

A muscle quivered in the woman's jaw as she glanced at Tom and back to Allison. Her eyes sparkled with amusement.

She knows she worries me. That pleases her, Allison thought.

"I have a reservation."

"We've been expecting you," Allison said. But instead of her usual handshake, she took a step back.

Tom looked at her and raised his eyebrows, then coughed. He turned to their guest. "I assume your bags are in your car."

The woman laughed. "I took a taxi and have only what I carry." She held up a carpet bag from another era.

"Well then, welcome to The Fair Lady," Tom said. "We're Allison and Tom McKinley." He offered his hand. "I'm afraid I don't remember your name."

The woman declined the handshake. "My name is Tunder-Liona Szepasszony, a Hungarian name. I am afraid it is hard to pronounce. You may call me Liona."

"Hungarian?" Allison's eyebrows raised. "We had a Hungarian guest. He passed away recently."

Liona removed her coat and handed it to Tom. "My uncle, Frederick Kalman. I came to the United States to visit him. Now I only collect his things."

"That's a relief," Allison said. "They're under the eaves in his bedroom. The room's vacant, I don't suppose . . ."

"I would be happy to have his room," Liona replied. "I will look into his possessions. Were there many?"

"Mostly clothes. I packed them away in a box."

Liona smiled at her, but it was a deceptive smile. It didn't reach her eyes. In fact, nothing reached her eyes. "I would be most grateful if you would show me to my room. Tonight, I am tired."

"Would you like something to eat first?" Allison asked, ready to feed her the roast beef left over from last night.

"No. Again, I am tired. I go to bed."

"I'll bring you up," Allison said.

Allison woke to a voice coming from the hall.

"Where is it?" Soft sobbing accompanied the words. "Where is it?"

Allison grabbed her robe and opened the door. Nobody. Except for the creaking's of an old house, nothing stirred. Shaking her head, she retreated and crawled back into bed.

"Anything else?" Allison was halfway out the door.

Tom shook his head and waved. "Babe, that about covers it."

Allison turned back to her husband and put her arms around his neck. "What will you do while I'm gone?"

Tom grinned. "Tackle the bookcase attacked by poltergeist last night."

Allison frowned. "It was fine yesterday. Wonder what happened." She kissed her husband and hurried out the door.

Tom studied the bookcase, trying to learn how the books could have been in such a mess and still stayed on the shelves. *Hungarian Folk Tales* fell into his hand. He replaced the book.

"Mr. McKinley." The voice came out of nowhere.

Tom spun around, dislodging another book. He held it in place with his back.

Liona.

"I cannot find a book belonging to my uncle. Maybe you know?"

He stared. Liona wore a white dress that appeared almost orange, reflected in the late afternoon sun.

Tom averted his eyes. "I wouldn't have a clue. Maybe my wife can help you."

Liona peered at the bookcase. "A book of Hungarian folktales. It is important to me—of sentimental value. A family treasure, you see."

Tom raised his eyebrows. He didn't know what to say. The folktales had been a gift from Frederick Kalman, and his wife loved the book. The name of their bed and breakfast was named in one of the tales. She'd been intrigued. He explained.

Behind her mask of smiles, Liona's eyes glowed with orange rage that almost matched the fiery sky.

A cold chill ran up his spine.

She said quietly, "I simply must have that book, Mr. McKinley. I'm willing to pay for it."

Tom stood his ground. "You'll have to ask my wife. I can't speak for her." The book against his back fell to the floor with a thud. The family Bible.

Liona moved closer, looked at the floor, frowned, and turned her head.

"I will." She left the room.

Tom stared after her, trying to figure out her sudden departure. He shook his head and put the Bible back next to *Hungarian Folk Tales.*

Christmas Eve. The traditional McKinley party—turning on the Christmas tree, eggnog spiked with rum, appetizers, dinner, and grab bag presents, finishing with Christmas carols.

But, as Allison sat to play Silent Night, Liona closed the hymnal.

"I sing you a song from my country." Instead of carols, she sang Hungarian Czardas and told fairy tales.

"You named your house after a fairy tale, did you not?" Liona asked Allison.

"No. The Fair Lady was already named."

"Do you know what a Fair Lady is?"

"A malevolent fairy," Allison replied. "A shapeshifter who can take animal and human form. A being tied to a household object. She can never leave it."

"Something like that," Liona replied softly. "The object is called her 'platter.' When the platter is taken from her, she will follow it to the ends of the earth. It is a danger for anyone keeping her from her home."

"Good one," a guest replied, who'd entered the room with a glass of eggnog, and mistletoe around his neck. He made for Liona.

A mask descended over the lady. Liona ducked under his outstretched arm and ran upstairs as the man waved the mistletoe in her face.

"Jushh havin' bit o' fun," the man slushed.

"I think you've had too much fun, dear," his wife replied.

But, while Tom was watching the retreating Liona, his wife was watching him. Suddenly, he felt a shadow covering his home. Something was very wrong.

A noise woke Tom. Snow blew against the window, then fluttered away. Allison lay sleeping on her side.

Again, the noise. Creaking on the stairs. Tom tiptoed halfway down and nearly fell the rest of the way. Liona lay naked on the floor, her black hair spilling onto the carpet. She held the book of fairy tales under the Christmas tree lights.

A gasp escaped from him. "What the hell do you think you're doing?" he whispered.

"I found it," she said, holding her book. "My platter, it is here. Now . . " She chanted, "You may come to me."

"No," he said.

"I command," she said.

Tom moved like a man possessed, but he felt air when he knelt and touched her skin.

Suddenly, without moving, she was standing. "Dance with me."

"No."

Hungarian music swept through the room. It came from nowhere and everywhere. In Liona's arms, either maneuvered by physical force or enchantment. He wasn't sure which.

"You take my home. Now you follow me into my world. Dance with me—come away with me."

They suddenly slipped through closed doors, onto the porch, and into the night.

"My God, you'll freeze to death," Tom said, half-frozen himself.

Her mind caught hold of his and whirled him onto the pathway through the snow. She showed no signs of the cold.

The silver slips of moonlight guided their steps. Even if he'd wanted to, he couldn't have stopped the frantic momentum built up by his phantom partner. Her shimmering body whirled him around and down the hill toward the river. And he gladly allowed himself to be caught up in her body, her movement, the music, and the mad side of his psyche.

On they whirled until they spun onto the ice on the river. And then, he fell through the ice. Bitter cold wrapped around his face. It was over, he thought. Over . . . over . . . over . . . But, his boots and clothing pulled him under.

Church bells pealed. Christmas Day. He came to his senses as the ice cracked around him.

"Angels we have heard on high . . ." The recessional of Midnight Mass.

He kept going down. He reached for disappearing hands as the freezing waters closed around him. Voices called out, *"Merry Christmas."*

This woman was leading Tom to his death. What was she? A witch from the depths of Hell? Damn her. He wasn't giving up without a fight.

"God help me!" He wasn't sure he was screaming or thinking. He went under and knocked his head on the ice, trying to come up for air. One last-ditch effort to catch those hands.

He succeeded. The hands held on and pulled him up---not Liona, but Allison.

They say tragedies run in threes. But love averted the third tragedy scheduled by the dislodged Fair Lady.

"Let's get you inside," Allison said softly. She slipped on something in the snow—the *Hungarian Folk Tales* with its pages open to *Fair Lady*, a folk tale of Hungary.

Allison and Tom stored the book in with the other things owned by the Hungarian guest--under the eaves in the attic of the church.

The Writers' Club Scandal

Revenge is as sweet as the most delicate wine.

Maurice, Kevin, William, and Jonathan sat in comfortable armchairs, forming a horseshoe in front of a stone fireplace centered on the short wall in Jonathan Butler's living room mansion. Tonight's Writers' Club topic was scandals. And as the members all agreed, there were plenty to fill many Writers' Club nights.

"You first, Kevin. What scandals do you have in your past?" The President of the club, Jonathan, directed his attention to toe-headed Kevin. He wondered which scandal his club secretary would share.

Kevin fidgeted in his chair. He stared at the ceiling and back down to the men. "Well, I did something, I guess, no writer should ever do."

"Ah, what's that?" Maurice asked, shuffling to the edge of his chair.

"I . . ." He shook his head. "No, I don't want to share that."

"Oh?" Jonathan asked. "Why not? We all have nastiness's to share."

Kevin appeared resigned. "Indeed, why not?" He cleared his throat. "You know that book of poetry I had published last spring?"

"Yeah," Jonathan said. And . . . ?"

"Well, I plagiarized it. From poor Clyde Griffin." Kevin stared at the floor for a second.

Jonathan said, "Damn, Kevin, we all knew that. You stole it from Clyde's files after his death. Glad you got it off your chest, though." He chuckled. "You don't think we all do that from time to time?"

"Maybe, but not a whole novel."

The four men nodded and exchanged furtive gazes.

Jonathan said, "Not to worry. Next up, William. What have you done wrong?"

"It was at a Writers' Conference, a couple of Junes ago. I wanted a position as a speaker of horror novels. They gave it to another guy. I snuck into the office, pulled his application, and took his name off the speaker list. Maybe, not too bad of a scandal. Bad enough, in my estimation. I was adequate. The other guy would have been better."

Maurice nodded. "Not too bad. Your insecurities will ruin you one of these days, though, William."

William said, "Yeah, I suppose they will." He smiled and said, "So, who's up next?"

Maurice said, "I volunteer."

Jonathan left the room briefly while Maurice got ready. When Jonathan came out, he brought a wine decanter with him.

The men's eyes focused on the wine.

Maurice said, "There was a time when I got Writers' Block. Couldn't think of anything to write—no creative juices. Like Kevin, I thought of Clyde immediately. So, I pilfered some of his writing material before the family could retrieve the files. Unlike Kevin, I didn't steal the whole thing. I've been adding this and that to my stories."

He didn't hang his head like Kevin. Instead, he grinned. "So there."

"You're next, Jonathan. We know you have skeletons in your closet," Maurice said. Jonathan was handing around a glass of Port served in elegant ruby wine glasses. He sat and gazed upon the other men.

"Okay, gentlemen. Do you remember your local history? The story about Maude Parker and Clyde Griffin?"

"Yes, of course. We were all around then."

The men looked at each other and shrugged. "What about it? It was a sad affair," Kevin said.

"Yes, it was," Jonathan said. "Maude was the belle of the town. She was engaged to Clyde but loved to play around. One night at a party, young Maude decided to flirt with Harry Brady. Clyde was furious and left in a huff. Later, he came back. He brought wine and offered it around. Everything seemed okay until some of the guests got deathly ill. Maude and Harry both died. Clyde was arrested."

"He was your uncle, wasn't he?"

"Yes."

"So, what happened?" They stared with rapt attention."

"Uncle Clyde was declared by physicians and law enforcement unfit to stand trial and committed to the Behavior Disorder Wing of the hospital. He never came out. Several years later, he died, completely insane.

"So, we come full circle. You all have a physician, lawyer, or police officer responsible for putting away dear Uncle Clyde. All of you are responsible."

The men appeared restless. Maurice grabbed his throat. Kevin hugged his stomach. William lost control of his breathing. A few minutes later, they lay on the floor, dead.

"May you rest in Hell!" Jonathan said before taking a large swig from the wine decanter. Then, he, too, lay on the floor with the rest of them.

Revenge is a dish best served cold, and the members of the Writers' Club were stone-cold . . . *dead.*

The Carousel

"The thing about taste, ladies and gentlemen, is its perceptions. Taste chooses the sweet, the salty and the sour, what clothes you wear, which household furnishings adorn your room, what colors you have on your walls." The barker reeled in his small but attentive public.

"Now, take this popcorn," he said, filling a paper bag with still popping popcorn. "You say this is salty? Tastes like corn? Tastes like the goodness of fresh butter?" The crowd looked at each other, shrugging their shoulders. They could smell the popcorn from the end of the Midway.

"Wrong!" bellowed the barker. "It tastes like the sweet flavor of vanilla ice cream." He handed it to a woman. She popped a kernel into her mouth, expecting the warmth of freshly popped popcorn. Instead, she put her hands up to her mouth, and her eyes grew wide.

"How did you do that?" The woman dove into the package and took out another piece to make sure. The crowd, bewildered and disbelieving, laughed.

In the background, the carousel circled around to a multitude of tunes. Kids laughed at the brightly colored horses on gold posts. "Get your ice-cold popcorn," the barker joked.

"The mind is an amazing thing, ladies and gentlemen," he continued. "You perceive this popcorn to be sweet, like ice cream? What if I tell you it's not? It's actually hot, like Chili Peppers." Several of his customers spat out their popcorn and fanned their mouths as though burned. "See? Perceptions."

He pointed toward a small building with a big-mouthed door. "Now playing, in our auditorium, 'The Mysterious Art of Hypnotism.' Step right up, ladies and gentlemen. See how normal people like you and me can change into other than what we are. Only ten dollars. Not much. Not much at all." They entered in droves, pushing to get inside.

As he turned, he bumped into Mr. Shade, the ambiguous carnival owner. He hadn't seen him standing there. No, he hadn't been there. How did he do that?

"Good turnout, Clydie," Mr. Shade said. "Very good." His dark eyes reflected into Clyde's. They became one and the same. "I think it's about time we put on those new horses, don't you?" On the outside stood three empty gold posts and behind it, a carriage.

Mechanically, Clyde nodded.

"You see the redheaded woman with the two children?" He pointed to the woman who'd eaten the ice cream popcorn.

"We need a red horse for the post and two smaller ponies to pull the carriage." He snapped his fingers about two inches from Clyde's face. Clyde's eyes pulled back into his head as though pulled by his brain, but then they sprang back to normal. He nodded and went through the back entrance.

"Hypnotize, to dazzle or overcome by suggestion. Who has not been hypnotized by the cunning of Madison Avenue? Today, you will see the power of hypnotism."

Clyde's short lecture was strangely powerful. The people came up, one by one, to perform funny acts. Before he worked as carnie, he'd been a psychologist, specializing in hypnotism. But the medical community expelled him as somewhat of a quack. This was his element.

The redheaded woman stepped onto the stage. Like the others, he put her in a trance from the simple, overplayed device of the ticking wristwatch. She was wonderfully suggestible. He made her neigh and made her dance like the carousel horses. He snapped his fingers.

"You will remember none of this," he whispered. "Come to the carousel at midnight. Bring your children." He snapped his fingers again, and the audience cheered.

On that clammy night, two boys escorted the woman toward the carousel. Mr. Shade and Clyde waited.

"What's going on?" she asked. "Why are we here?"

Clyde pointed to the carousel as haunting music rose from its bowels.

"Step right up. Ride the carousel."

The mother and two children stepped onto the carousel. That was their first and last mistake. The carousel catapulted into action. It whirled slowly, then faster and faster, until the human eye could no longer see the distinction of the finely crafted horses. In the calm night air, the carousel became a tornado.

Clyde Shadows solicited his public in front of the grand carousel. Today, one new red horse and two ponies filled the gold posts.

"The thing about taste, ladies and gentlemen, is that there are so many perceptions."

Mr. Shade turned his back on the crowd and disappeared.

Demons of the Writing Mind

*A writer's urgency to finish her short story
about a wife who wants to end her life.*

Lucille stood on the Dunes, looking over the peacefulness and tranquility of Lake Michigan. It was hot, and Lucille did not feel neither peaceful nor tranquil. She was on the run.

A couple of lovers walked hand in hand. They noticed her and walked away, looking for a more secluded spot. She smiled. This was one place the *police wouldn't think to look, and if they did? So, what? She'd throw herself over before they were within one hundred yards. She knew that was what would happen anyway.*

"Crap!" I said, not at all ladylike. "What the devil would a woman really feel like if she had just killed her husband and was about to pitch herself over a cliff?" I stamped my foot and walked into the kitchen, deciding to do the dishes from last night. "Demons, my foot!" I slammed the Corelle dish a little too hard on the counter, and it broke. "Damn! *Damn!* Corelle's are not supposed to break. Calling out for pizza, I guess."

"Okay, here goes. Brain! Get in gear!"

She knew she couldn't have taken any more abuse. Every afternoon, George would stop for a "quick one." The "quick one" usually turned into a "long one," and George couldn't handle his liquor. Usually, glassy-eyed, he came home and picked a fight. The fight turned into a slamming match. She had black eyes and bruised arms as proof.

"I wonder how that feels?" I punched my arm and winced. Do writers really need to live the experiences of their characters? God, I hope not. I got up and went into the bedroom to make my bed. My mind kept floating back and forth, back and forth: clean the house, mow the lawn, write, study my grammar, train the dogs, write, do my lesson plans for school, write, read a *good* book, write. I continued my thousand-word short story.

George had been blind drunk the previous evening, and his demons didn't even bother picking a fight. They went directly for the baseball bat. Lucille tripped him, and as he cursed, she hit him over the head at least ten times.

"Good for her, the lousy . . ." Well, maybe not ten times, and would he still be cursing after the first blow? Shoot, time to feed the dogs. I got up and poured Nutri-Max (not intended as a commercial) into their bowls. "Shit," I said. "Really glad I'm single."

Back to the story.

It had been strange sleeping in her bed alone with George lying dead downstairs. An experience she wouldn't want to repeat. She wouldn't need to repeat. Her mind corrected the error. By nightfall, she, too, would be dead. Would she have to spend eternity with George?

"God! I hope not. How is she going to get out of this?" So far, I've had some four hundred words in my story. I had demons in my soul, too. They consisted of a thousand-word short story once a week. I had two more hours to complete my assignment and desperately needed a Diet Cream Soda.

It was now approaching noon. Lucille wished she had brought out her Sunblock 24 as the sun beat down. She . . .

I realized that it was I that needed sunglasses and Sunblock 24. Though it was fast approaching sunset, the sun was setting directly into the kitchen window and causing little flashing demons of light on my monitor. I had trouble reading the screen through the glare.

"Grocery shopping! I have to go grocery shopping!" Those mind demons again.

Lucille opened the picnic basket and spread her lunch out on the elegant lace tablecloth she and George received for their last anniversary.

Would she really have the presence of mind to make a picnic lunch? Good, God! My lawn needs mowing! Oh jeez, only six hundred words! How am I going to get her out of this?

The lunch having been consumed . . .

Sounds like a bad Nineteen-Century Victorian Romance novel. Speaking of romance, how about a love interest?

The evening sun went down in a final blaze of glory as Lucille realized her last evening on earth. It was a wonderful send-off. The colors of peaches, oranges, yellows all mingled with violets, and blues and clouds flickered their steely, grey tones adding to the painting. She thought it might rain.

Speaking of rain, did I shut my bedroom windows? The glare in the monitor suddenly disappeared, and I heard a crack of thunder. How appropriate! Only a half-hour left until six o'clock and the change of topics!

She looked down onto the beach. It had to be hundreds of feet below, and the rocks would make sure of a swift death . . . Of her quick death.

What was that sound? She turned and looked down the path that led back into the forest preserves—the sound of a motor, she trembled, they'd found her. They would charge her with murder and put her on trial. She would be executed or spend an excruciating rest of her life behind bars. Death wouldn't be so bad, but to spend the next ten years waiting for it, she couldn't take that.

"Alex, I wonder what it would feel like to spend the next ten years on Death Row?" Alex is my blue-merle collie. He yawned, and I looked at the clock. Five minutes to go.

"Wait, Lucille."

That voice. It was (What would his name be? Alex. That's it!) *It was Alex. The man she should have married!*

"Don't! Lucille, we know what happened! Your neighbor saw him through the open door. She knows it was self-defense!"

She stood, mesmerized, by the sound of his voice. Then, they ran to each other without a word and stood, locked in an embrace for a very long time.

"Really dumb, but whew! Got her out of that one! How many words? No! It's over eleven hundred. Two minutes left. Jeez, what am I going to remove?" For the next minute, I deleted words.

"Finally! Exactly nine hundred ninety-nine! Now, press 'select all,' 'copy' and (Hm! Hurry *up* AOL) Okay! Got it! 'Paste!' Now hit 'submit'—okay! Got it!"

That was before I discovered the typos!

Silent Night, Deadly Night

A wife leaves a mental facility to return to her husband and daughter. But, who's the one who needs to be in the mental facility?

The silence was deafening. Susan Morrison put her hands to her ears to ward off the deathly stillness of the night. The gun—a Saturday Night Special, given to her by her brother weighed her pocket. She felt the pumping . . . no, pounding of her heart. Cold sweat poured down her face. What had happened? Where had it all gone so tragically wrong? Her friends said he was the perfect husband. One minute their relationship was more incredible than she could ever have dreamed. The next . . . well, bizarre things started to happen. Minor accidents became more significant accidents—Linda nearly falling out the window. Then somehow, the gas oven leaking all that gas. She almost had been killed that time. Had the oven been left on intentionally? Somehow, was she to blame? A noise jolted her back to reality. She turned. Nothing. Something far away shattered the peacefulness of the evening. It was just a foghorn blasting from the lighthouse warning off ships that were coming into the harbor. She breathed a sigh of relief.

She wanted to get back into the house but knew she couldn't. *He* was in there. In there with Linda, her little girl. What would he do to her? She had to get back inside. Had to wrench her daughter away from the madman she called her husband. She tiptoed up to the back porch avoiding the autumn leaves lying strewn around the path. She stopped and listened. Nothing.

Slowly and carefully, she walked up the porch steps. Crouching, she lowered herself down beneath the window. She peered in. Linda was sitting on the couch watching television holding the stuffed bear she had given her two years ago. That had been her first birthday present. She stifled the cry that came from somewhere inside.

Her heart raced and skipped a beat. Her husband sat opposite Linda, holding something in his hand. What was that . . . a knife? *My God!* What was he going to use that for? Run Linda! Get out of there! Linda didn't move. She kept watching the television screen and eating . . . popcorn. She was much too young to understand. Susan dared not breathe for fear of discovery. Could her little girl be eating . . . poisoned popcorn?

Wait . . . there was someone else in the room with them. A woman was coming out of the kitchen. She wore all white. Could he be in this together with someone else . . . have an accomplice? Better be careful, she thought. Kidnaping was a capital offense. She could be in grave danger. She rubbed her eyes, so full of tears and her heart, so full of fear. She looked again. Standing next to the woman in white stood another man. He was dressed casually in a beige sport coat contrasting a pair of navy pants. He held a pad in his hand. He was taking notes. Who were these people?

Susan started to hyperventilate. Steering her daughter away from one kidnapper, her father at that, was one thing. But, trying to get her away from three was something else. She needed to come up with a plan. She thought about racing in and holding them at gunpoint while she grabbed Linda. No. Too risky.

Maybe she could create a diversion outside. While they were occupied, she could sneak in the front and race Linda out of there. But what? She eyed the kerosene lamp that had always been kept on the back porch table. Did she have any matches? She felt in her pocket and realized that she had put a pack in her pocket when she was at the restaurant.

What could she light? She didn't want the whole house to go up in flames. The storage shed—perfect. They kept the lawnmower and other gardening tools back there. What else? Oh yes, the rags—rags to clean up spills, usually of gasoline. That would do. Susan crept silently over to the kerosene lamp and tiptoed back over to the shed. Fumbling around in the dark, she felt for the pack of matches.

The rags on the floor were soaked in turpentine from last month's paint project. "Yes, here they are." She took them out and lit one.

Susan wasn't prepared for the reaction caused by that match.

The shed exploded more violently than she could even imagine. Susan didn't get much chance to imagine anything. The blast killed her instantly.

Douglas Morrison heard the explosion and reacted first.

"My God! What's that?" He raced to the back, followed by Mia Lloyd and George Rogers, medical professionals at the Beaver State Mental Hospital.

"Susan! No! My God, Susan!" was all Doug could get out when they found the charred remains of his wife.

"Uh, Mr. Morrison?"

He looked up as the Chief of Police, Robert Wilton, came over to him. "You know this was set deliberately?"

"You mean . . . Susan?" He shook his head in disbelief.

Mia Lloyd put her hand on his shoulder. "I'm so sorry, Mr. Morrison. So very sorry. She was very paranoid, you know. Ever since she escaped, this has been our biggest fear . . . that she would come back here and try to take Linda. She was so sure you would hurt her. She was, well, delusional. Maybe it's better this way."

Douglas looked at Mia and shook his head. "Better?"

"Well, better for her. We're not entirely sure what afflicted her, but her condition seemed to be getting worse. No telling what she might have done if she had taken Linda. I'm so sorry."

"Night, Daddy."

Douglas sat on the edge of Linda's bed, tucking her in and trying to soothe his frightened daughter. He thought that it was a good thing she was too young to understand what had happened.

"Night precious."

Douglas ambled back downstairs and out onto the back porch. The night was silent except for a few seagulls overhead. He could still smell the smoke, but it was now mingling with the scent of the pines and the night air.

He took it all in and started to giggle. It was a small giggle at first, but then it came in twos, then threes, then like waves spilling out of him like crashes from the ocean.

"*Ding dong, the witch is dead!*" he screamed at the silence. "The *bitch* is dead! I managed to convince them she was crazy, and now she managed to kill *herself*. I didn't even have to do it for her!"

Ice Cream Sundaes and Ice Cold Murder

A family discovers the heartbreak of drive-by shootings.
I wrote this while I was teaching school in the inner city of Chicago.

Seven-year-old Dante Banks sat on the stoop listening to his grandpa telling the same old Saturday night stories for the past five years. Grandpa would go down to the old corner store on sweltering summer nights and pick up ice cream. Sometimes he'd bring back cones. Other times, it would include fudge sauce and whipped cream. Grandpa would go in and shoe away Grandma from the kitchen, and he'd make ice cream sundaes. Dante's mouth watered as he waited patiently for Grandpa to come to a break.

Gunshots blasted in the distance. The noise startled Dante, and as he jerked his head back, his baseball cap came loose on his head and flopped to one side. His Grandma quickly turned it back the way it was.

"Why did you do that for?"

His Grandma nervously looked at her husband and then replied, "It looks better that way, honey. That's all. Keep it that way for Grandma."

Dante made a face.

"Baby, please," his grandfather replied. "Look, when you wear your hat that way, well, that's a sign that you belong to the Blue Devils. They wear their hats that way. Any other gang will look at you as their enemy, even at your age. It's not safe, honey."

It wasn't as though Dante was scared. Oh no! Not him! He'd heard about the gang wars and listened to the gangs firing at each other every summer since he was born. He was used to it. He did notice his grandma nudge just a tad closer to Grandpa each time she heard it, and he didn't like it when Grandma was frightened. He wondered if that might have something to do with the death of his parents when he and Tiffany were just babies. They called it a "drive-by." His parents hadn't been gang members.

"Where's it coming from tonight, Grandpa?" Dante's sister, Tiffany, changed the subject.

"I guess maybe from over Madison Avenue somewhere," Grandpa said.

Dante noticed that Grandpa usually never stopped telling his stories when he heard gunfire. He just kept right on going on even when the firing seemed to get louder. He heard police sirens droning in the background. This time, Grandpa surprised Dante and stopped the story.

"Well, children, how about a nice ice cream sundae? Yes sir! It's too hot for any more storytelling now. Whew, it's so hot I could fry an egg on the stoop!" He laughed, and the kids laughed with him. "Now then, two scoops of ice cream, one chocolate, and one vanilla, with lots of fudge sauce . . . hot, of course. Then the best, fresh whipped cream anyone could ask for." He smiled in anticipation. Dante thought that the anticipation was as much for Grandpa as it was for him and Tiffany. Dante really loved his grandpa.

"Why don't we all come inside?" Grandpa reached for the screen door, but his attention wasn't entirely focusing on the children. His eyes seemed to gaze somewhere out toward Madison Street.

"No! Oh, Grandpa, it's so hot out and even hotter inside. Can't we stay outside?" Tiffany sniffled and batted her baby eyelashes. Dante took up her cause. "Yeah, can't we, huh?" He wanted to be outside where the action was.

"Okay, okay," said Grandpa, resigned. He went inside alone.

They waited patiently outside, watching the neighbors watering their lawns, sweeping sidewalks, and talking. Grandma would wave, and they'd wave back, then go about their business. Occasionally, they would look up the block. For what? He noticed Mrs. Hill and Mr. Martins talking to the Smiths. He saw them look down the block and then go abruptly into their houses. He wondered why.

"Here we are," came a big booming voice from inside. Grandma got up and went inside to help Grandpa. When they came out, Grandpa held a child's version of heaven on a tray. It displayed four whopping ice cream sundaes surrounded by chocolate chip cookies. Grandpa beamed with delight at the look on the children's faces.

"Wow!" Dante and Tiffany said simultaneously. Dante's hat fell off his head again. He picked it up and scrunched it onto his head so that the front of the cap perched sideways. Each child picked their sundaes, took a cookie, and went back to sit on the stoop.

Dante thought it strange all the neighbors had gone inside on such a beautiful night and didn't notice a black car cruising down the street. It slowed as it came to the middle of the block and appeared to be looking for something. The car seemed to have an independent mind without drivers and controls. First, it would speed up, and then it would slow down . . . speed up, slow down. It came to Dante's house, where he was munching on his cookie, and stopped. The window opened.

"Can you tell me where Monroe Street is?" A figure called to him from inside the car. Before Grandpa could stop him, Dante popped off the stoop and skipped down toward the car.

"Sure . . ."

Dante never got out another sound. The human face seemed to instantly turn into metal and steel, which started pummeling bullets into the happy, smiling face of Dante Banks. His little baseball cap went flying for one final time.

The next day the headlines read, *Another Child Killed in West Side, Drive-By Shooting.*

Three Gold Balls

Richard Hollingsway stood behind the counter of his pawnshop, 'The Three Gold Balls,' as he did every day. His was a very special pawnshop.

Oh, there was the usual array of jewelry. In the case beneath the counter, the typical rings, bracelets, necklaces lay abandoned, and unwanted musical instruments such as trumpets, guitars, and saxophones decorated the shop walls.

Ladies would bring in their furs, each having two purposes—money and desperation.

Richard Hollinsway tried to bring a little peace to those who came. Take, for instance, the suffering freelance artist, Mrs. Roberts. Instantly, Mr. Hollinsway knew she was the right kind of customer.

She'd brought in a mink coat. She needed enough money to pay her rent and—*just a little extra?*

"Just a little extra?" He asked.

"Just a bit to get me back on my feet."

Mr. Hollinsway mentioned his price, and Mrs. Roberts reluctantly agreed.

Mrs. Roberts, it turned out, struck it rich when her paintings suddenly began to sell, and she became famous. Oh . . . all she had to pawn was her mink and her soul.

She was able to buy back the mink.

The Lighthouse

Do you believe lighthouses can be evil?

"Miranda. There it is!" Martin McGovern steered his boat around the alcove and into full view of a tall white lighthouse with red circles plastered from the foot of the structure to the top. That beauty guarded the rocky coast of Devil's Bay.

Strange, they hadn't seen it before. Miranda was awestruck by its beauty. They should have seen this towering structure for miles. She guessed that the overhang of the rocks and cliffs blocked the view. She gasped.

"Oh, Marty! The lighthouse. It's so big!" was all she could get out. The pounding of the surf behind them made it impossible to hear his response. The sky grew darker, but it was hard to tell because of the closeness of the cliffs. A crack of thunder, soft at first, then louder, then—ear-splitting.

"Marty, I think it's going to rain!"

"Ye . . . up."

"Uh . . . The waves . . . Look at them!"

"Tell me something I don't know. We're almost there," Marty said, a growl coming into his voice.

The waves grew larger and tossed the boat,

Martin was already pulling the boat into the small dock which led up to the lighthouse. As Miranda got out, the approaching storm clouds covered up the rays of the sun. It created an overcast of shadows and . . . what? She suddenly felt a chill. Was something wrong? Something about this building. A shadow seemed to surround—engulf it. A wave knocked Miranda off her seat and nearly overboard. She grabbed the side of the boat and stayed on her feet.

"Come on, Miranda. Hurry!" Marty got out of the boat and grabbed both her hands.

Miranda fell over the side and onto the dock—with a look toward the lighthouse. "Hurry, damn it."

"But Marty . . ." She didn't finish.

He opened the ground door and pushed her inside.

Miranda started to protest.

"Marty?"

Marty's eyes turned red. His grin grew sharp pointed teeth. "Have fun, darling. I think you'll enjoy this little adventure." With that, he disappeared through the portal to the outside.

The door slammed and locked. Miranda was inside the place she'd wanted to come to for years. She stepped toward the door and stopped, staring at the empty space where Marty had been seconds ago. With that, the door slammed shut and locked. She was in . . ."

In front of her . . . behind her . . . only darkness. What was this . . . this *place*? Her heart raced with the thoughts of where she could be. *Hell?* What had she done so wrong that she deserved this? Then, she remembered all the evil things she'd done. The thefts . . . the abuse . . . the . . . wickedness, all the things she'd done, the people she'd hurt, the animals she'd abused. Maybe she could make up all the wrongs she'd done?

"It's too late for you, Miranda. So, come in," said an echoing voice. "We've been waiting for you."

As Marty pulled away from the lighthouse, he read the sign above the front door: *Abandon hope, all ye who enter here.*

"She's in for it now," he said, grinning, as he motored his boat toward a calm, open sea. His eyes no longer glared red; his teeth straightened.

No more lightning. Thunder gone. He chuckled. Another soul going into the depth of *Hell.*

Now, for the next victim.

Green River

In the Green River cabins, tenants come and tenants disappear.
They all have green in their names.

Mr. Ward Greene took down the 'For Rent' sign in front of the beautiful white cottage with green shutters. Even though the house looked small, a wrap-around porch was ideally situated around its perimeter. The path down to the dock where the Green River flowed gave the place an extra incentive for a potential buyer.

"This cottage belonged to the famous horror writer, Edward Green Bryant," the owner explained to Mr. and Mrs. Greenbrier, his new "perfect" tenants.

Mrs. Greenbrier wore dark green jeans, a matching green shirt, and a lighter green tank top. "Whatever happened to him?" Mrs. Greenbrier asked. "I used to love his stories. You know he always set them near the Green River?"

"Wonder where he got all those great ideas." Mr. Greenbrier looked around at the surrounding fields that backed into a forest and then the river. The grass, fields, and trees matched Mrs. Greenbriar's outfit.

"Probably from that river, Dad," ten-year-old Jeffrey said, pointing. "Our river?" he asked, pulling his dad's sleeve hopefully.

"Well, I don't know, son. Maybe. Let's go look inside, shall we?"

"They say it's haunted," eight-year-old Hillary said. She included "Oooo" and made ghost gestures. "You know I love a good ghost story."

"They say, in the dark, it glows *green*." Jeffrey seemed excited about having his own haunted river in his front yard. He loved ghost stories, too.

"Maybe ghosts pulled Mr. Bryant into the river," his dad said. He laughed.

Mr. Ward grimaced and shook his head. "Not seen any ghosts around here. Not since…"

"Not since?" Mrs. Greenbriar asked, but she was cut off by her oldest.

"Can we have Mr. Ward over to tell ghost stories? Huh? Can we *please*?" Jeffrey asked, pleading.

"Can you tell us the story of the Green River? And about what happened to Mr. Bryant? Was he hacked to pieces by a nasty ghost?" Jeffrey jumped up and down, his hand shaking Mr. Ward's arm.

"Where did you get that idea?" Mr. Ward asked, raising his eyebrows. "Ah, the neighbors, of course." He nodded. "Tonight might just be the perfect night." Mr. Ward confirmed his invitation with Jeffrey's parents.

"We'd love to have you over, "Mrs. Greenbriar said, smiling into the gracious hostess role.

Eight o'clock found Mr. Ward and the Greenbriars sitting on green wicker chairs on the unscreened back porch of their cottage. They were all enjoying themselves, drinking coffee and eating Mr. Ward's chocolate cake as they listened to him gossip and tell stories.

Chirping crickets and fluttering birds trying to settle for the night contrasted the stillness of the evening. The river reflected a silvery full moon and the lights from the other side of its banks. An occasional fish plopped out of the water, causing ripples. Green tinted its darkness.

"It's true," Mr. Ward said. "There is a legend about this river. There have been century-old ghost tales about the Green River. They say that revolutionary soldiers massacred an entire Indian tribe right here. A child named Green River fled into the river chased by the soldiers and, in a panic, screamed a curse at the soldiers and drowned. Since then, every August, the river avenges her, and people with green in their names disappear."

Little Hillary and Jeffrey stared at him wide-eyed.

"*That's* why it's called Green River. It's only a legend." Mr. Ward smiled and stared out over the water.

They sat in silence until he continued.

"Sometimes," he whispered, "in August, you can picture the river turning green."

As he formed the mental image, Mr. Greenbrier swore a green haze floated onto his wife and kids, turning them green and translucent. He looked at his arm. Horrified, he could see straight through to the floor.

As his family faded, Mr. Greenbrier saw another presence. Rising from the river, an apparition, translucent and green, beckoned—Edward Green Bryant.

A smiling Mr. Ward put up the "For Rent" sign in front of the beautiful white cottage with green shutters.

He'd settle for nothing less than just the right tenants.

A car pulled into his driveway. A man, woman, and little boy emerged. Each wore something green.

The Legion of the Black Rose

*This short story is the story that started my journey
and later morphed into **Legacy of Danger**.*

It wasn't every day a girl received a castle for Christmas.

Elena Dkany, Alexander Brancusi, his sister, Marina, and her husband, Peter, stared wide-eyed at the family's Romanian solicitor and uncle, Gregory Balogh.

Uncle Gregory had been the conversational center since he'd introduced himself at Elena's aunt's funeral. He placed his hands in a prayer motion and looked apologetic.

"Elena, I have two gifts that have been locked up in the Dkany Castle vault. They should have been presented to you years ago." He reached over into his briefcase and pulled out two gift-wrapped boxes, one square and one long and narrow.

"Oh—" Elena brightened but was surprised.

Uncle Gregory handed her the gifts, and she fingered the packages. She opened the square one first and took out the most beautiful silver engraved jewel box she'd ever seen. The detail on the figures of fifteenth-century Boyars on horseback was so accurate Elena guessed silversmiths created it in that era.

"Oh Gregory," Elena said, almost breathless, "this is exquisite."

"It is so," Gregory said, his eyes shining. His tone lowered to a whisper. "But look inside." The penetration from his eyes narrowed like a beam to the box.

"Elena, this has been in safekeeping for you since your parents died," Gregory said. "Open it."

When she opened the case, what she saw sent her into momentary shock.

A dark, fiery, blood-red ruby lay on a backdrop of white velvet. Intersecting needles joined in the center of the stone displaying a luminous star. It looked ancient and rare.

"My God," Elena murmured, fingering the stone. "A star ruby. The color of blood . . ." She looked up. "And passion."

Alex raised his head at that moment and look into her eyes.

She looked away.

"The color of blood," Alex replied. Everyone turned to him.

"No, definitely . . . passion," Marina said, nestled in Peter's arms on the floor. She looked at her husband and flashed him a crooked smile.

"Yes . . . it's breathtaking," Elena said, rising and holding it against the light, entranced. It seemed to cast a fiery eye at her.

All of a sudden, a burning sensation crossed her palm like the stone contained hot coals. "Oh . . ." Elena dropped the ruby into Alex's outstretched hand.

"What's wrong?" he asked.

"I saw . . . saw something watching me from its intersection." She looked up and saw everyone staring at her. Shaking her head, she said, "I know how crazy that must seem to you, but . . ."

"Yes, I can see how you could form that impression. The stone has a magnificent center to it," Uncle Gregory said.

Alex fingered the stone, caressing it gently, moving his finger back and forth over its cool surface. The gentleness of his touch wasn't lost on Elena.

"It's a beautiful piece . . . magnificent," Uncle Gregory said. His voice trailed off, and he seemed far away.

Gregory cleared his throat and took the stone from Alex. Placing it between two bony fingers, he held it into the light. "I think this stone has been in existence since the beginning of the Orthodox Church in Romania," he said, procuring everyone's attention.

"In Romania, in the town of Dkany, there stood a monastery famous for its wealth. The story goes that it was plundered by the Turks through the spoils of war. Priceless jewels from India encrusted a magnificent silver cross that proudly stood on the altar." Gregory seemed to go into a trance.

"The power in Romania kept switching back and forth. Prince Vlad-Tepes, who you all probably know as the model for the Dracula stories, actually ruled in Transylvania. He killed thousands, which he either burned alive or impaled, leaving them to suffer horrific agonies. Occasionally, he'd be so proud of himself, he'd have dinner brought out to the dying field. He watched them die as he dined.

Elena groaned at Uncle Gregory's description.

"Vlad-Tepes had other enemies besides the Turks," he continued. "The conspiracies surrounding him made him paranoid. He impaled several monks for expressing moral indignation about the number of deaths he caused. Not too many dared oppose him.

"The Legion of the Black Rose emerged, led by Viktor Dkany, head of the Dkany dynasty. They'd been close friends of the prince until his insane behavior became impossible. In a battle with the Turks in 1476, Viktor struck down and killed Vlad-Tepes. Out of gratitude for his service, the church chiseled out the ruby from the altar cross and presented it to him."

"My God," whispered Elena. "You mean this ruby dates back to the fifteenth century?"

"Probably older," Gregory replied. "Remember, the Turks possessed it first."

"Why the secrecy all these years?" Elena asked.

"Before he died, Vlad-Tepes put a curse on the Dkany family. The black rose came to symbolize the league's treachery. He swore any member of the family who came in contact with the black rose would die."

"But that's just a legend, isn't it? There aren't really any black roses, are there?" Marina asked.

Peter answered. "They do, but they're rare. Their legend suggests retaliation and vengeance."

"There's something else," Gregory said. "Before your parents died, Elena, they received an anonymous package on your mother's twenty-first birthday. Inside the package was a black silk rose. Soon after, your mother contracted pneumonia and died. Your father killed himself, shortly after, of a broken heart . . . I think."

Elena wondered if her girlish romantic fantasy about true love and a death sacrifice to be with the one you loved stemmed from her father's suicide.

"I was here at the time," Gregory said. "When I heard she was so ill, I came to the states to see if I could be of any help."

"A coincidence, maybe? Pneumonia can be fatal," Elena said, hoping for more information.

"It could be a coincidence, maybe—maybe not."

"That's just a legend, isn't it?" Alex asked, crossing his arms, challenging. "You don't know the deaths in the Dkany family have all been preceded with black roses, do you?"

"No, of course not. But Viktor's wife received a black rose and died shortly after her twenty-first birthday—poisoned. They found the murderer, a follower of Vlad-Tepes, and although consensus thought it well deserved, no one envied his fate. Several years later, another Dkany lady received a rose. She died shortly after her twenty-first birthday. Another one. With some evidence of foul play, her death also was attributed to the curse. But since then, there have been no black roses or strange deaths that I know of, until your mother."

"What does the ruby have to do with it? I thought the church gave it to Viktor as a reward," Elena said.

"It was thought to have protective powers."

"It didn't protect my mother," Elena remarked.

"Where's the cross, now?" Alex asked.

"On display in a church in Bucharest," Gregory replied. The good friars managed to hide it during the years of communism."

"This ruby is truly wonderful," Elena said, "But shouldn't it be returned to the church?

"No. The church gave it to Viktor in grateful appreciation." Gregory remained solemn, then still, and a hush fell over the group.

"Anyone want a drink?" Peter asked, breaking the silence and rising to his feet. "I need one."

"No, wait," Gregory said. "I would like Elena to open the other package. For myself, I am curious. This was to be presented to you when you received the ruby."

Elena opened the silver gift wrapping and stared at a thin, long box. "I hope this isn't a black rose. Any other color would be nice." But an apprehension and foreboding again wound their combined tentacles down Elena's spine. "My God. I'm twenty-one today."

"Don't worry, Elena. It's only a legend," Marina said.

Uncle Gregory looked away.

When Elena finally found the courage to open it, she tried to grab hold of something. Still, suddenly the room started to spin, and the ground came rushing up toward her. She fell into Alex's outstretched arms and let the black silk rose fall at his feet before the sunset light disappeared.

No Way Out

" It says, 'No Way Out,' Michael." Carrie Llewellyn pointed at a sign. "But, honey, there has to be."

"Why?" Carrie's eyes still sparkled with the light of a newlywed. She gave him a crooked smile.

"Wait." Michael looked at the entrance sign and back to what he thought should have been the exit sign. "Maybe it's 'round back."

He picked up the larger of the two suitcases and started to walk down the large aisle moving around the milling crowds of people who made their way onto the train platforms. Carrie picked up the remaining bag and followed her husband.

"Mike, wait!" She had trouble keeping up.

"Sir, can you tell me where the exits are? We just went to the main entrance, but the exits are blocked off."

A man in a grey flannel suit looked at the pair and smiled. It was benign but sorrowful.

"Yee-ss," he drawled. His high cheekbones and ashen pallor gave Carrie a nervous feeling in the pit of her stomach—sort of like pitching waves.

The man pointed down a long, dark hall flooded with a mass of humanity. They started down the aisle dodging people who seemed to move in slow motion.

"God! Don't these people have anywhere to go?" Michael stopped, and his wife nearly pushed him over. The aisle seemed to get longer and longer.

"Mike!" Carrie grabbed Mike's arm. She stopped in her tracks and pointed to the sign by the door.

"No Exit"

"Jeez! Now what?" Michael came to the end of his rope as he sat on his suitcase and let out a puff of air.

"Can't we just exit anyway? Go out the entrance?" They watched as a few people entered the large doors, which separated the station from the outside world. Carrie walked over to the entrance and nearly got run down as a flood of people poured in.

"Guess not," She went back to Michael. "This is spooky."

Michael stood up and went over to a young woman. "Miss, can you tell me how we get out of here?"

He stared at a skeleton of a woman looking back at him. Her pallid skin seemed to encase a too-small frame with eyes so huge that seemed totally out of proportion. Her children looked emaciated.

"There's no way out of here, sir," she said simply. She gave a slight sorrowful glance toward Carrie, didn't say another word, and continued on her way.

"Wait! Miss!"

"Michael. She looked like death!" Carrie shivered as she huddled toward Michael. "What is this place?"

"Now, don't you start! This is a train station, Carrie. Just a plain train station. That's *all*. Come on. There's probably an exit on the other side of the platforms."

Michael hurried along, not wanting Carrie to see the scared look on his face. This was just bad management, bad planning on the City's part. Typical. He'd write to the mayor . . . Call the Governor's office. He passed the train on which they'd arrived. The dent on the front of the engine where it rammed into the side of that empty boxcar stood out like an angry gash—a frightening experience. Luckily, no one was injured. He saw the conductor change the destination signs. He hurried past, somehow feeling sorry for the emptiness of the train. He didn't know why.

He passed another conductor putting up another destination sign. This time Michael stopped and stared. There was no writing on the sign. It just had a simple arrow. The arrow pointed down. He tried to get the conductor's attention, but the man just stared past him.

"Michael, let's go . . ." Carried tugged at his sleeve and pointed at the sign. "Wait, Michael, what does that mean?"

"Carrie, I don't know. I can't get anyone to answer my questions."

They saw a swarm of people loading onto the train. The conductor seemed to be checking off a list. Some people—he turned away and pointed in another direction. They seemed relieved. They saw another swarm of people unloading from another train and moving in their direction. Some were pleading, some were crying.

"There's no escape," a man said, shaking his head at Michael as he walked by.

"No escape from what?" There was no answer.

"Sir?" Michael walked up to the conductor, an official who looked like he was past ninety. "Am I on some kind of passenger list? Is there such a thing?"

"Son, you're not on my list."

"So, there is a list. Where is this train going?"

"You haven't figured it out yet?"

"Figured what out?" Despite himself, Michael started to sweat. He felt a numbing, tingling sensation in his feet. His head began to swirl with surreal thoughts.

"Son, move away. You go to that train over there."

"But I'm coming from Southport. I'm trying to find the exit to the street."

"There is no exit onto the street, son."

What do you mean?" Michael was nearly screaming now. Carrie stood by, watching in alarm.

"Son, you remember that accident you had on the train?"

"Yeah, so?"

The conductor pointed to a paper in a nearby newspaper rack. The headlines read: "Train Crashes in Southport. All passengers killed."

"*No!*"

"*Oh, Michael, no. You mean . . . we're . . . dead?*"

Michael nodded and held onto Carrie's waist. "Yes. We are. Come on, Carrie. Let's get on the train."

Slowly, Michael and Carrie let themselves be carried in the direction of the train on the opposite platform. The one with the dent.

The destination pointed up.

Maggie's Fallen Heroes

Are all the reportedly deceased soldiers really dead?

"Ashes to ashes, dust to dust…"

Maggie stood in the front of the crowd watching her father being lowered into the earth. At least, he'd been given a hero's exit. In life, he'd been just another miner working himself to death for the established oligarchy. She was a coal miner's daughter and proud of it. The fact that her family had been snubbed all her life gave her a defiant air and a flash to her green eyes. Now that she was enormously successful, she could have snubbed her nose at the most prominent of people.

With the red hair, who looked gorgeous in blues and greens, Maggie wore black in the old tradition. She stood shivering not from the cold but from grief. The death of Richard, her own fallen hero, some thirty years ago had changed her life forever. With her mother's death last year, and now her father, the only one left was her son, Mark.

Bagpipes fanned out around the grave, softly playing "Amazing Grace." A minister from the tiny Pennsylvania Church read the Burial Rites. She couldn't help the lump that went all the way from the pit of her stomach up into her throat, ending up in a river of tears. Mark put his arm around her.

She turned and glanced at him. He looked like her, but not quite. His hair was lighter, reddish-blond and his eyes were bright blue. She thought that he had his father's profile. Except for some pictures of the dashing Richard Langdon, visual memories of her fallen hero had faded, but not the memories from her heart—never those.

"Did you find it?" Maggie whispered.

"I found the plaque."

"Yes, and . . . ?"

"His name wasn't on it."

"Our father, who are in heaven . . ."

"Mark, it has to be there," she whispered.

"Shh," someone whispered.

"Leave them alone," A man whispered back.

Maggie was grateful, and the crowd pushed in behind her.

"Hallowed be thy name . . ."

"Mom, I'm telling you his name isn't on that plaque. Could he still be alive?"

Maggie felt his arm on her shoulder and stifled a sob of new possibilities. Could that be?

She would never forget that phone call, not ever.

"Maggie? I'm so sorry to tell you this, but our son, Richard, was killed. Sorry, we couldn't get to you before this. We only got the news a couple of weeks ago. It's been very hard on us. You'll be happy to know that we had a memorial in his honor last week."

Maggie had been shut out, dismissed like a family servant.

"Mom. We have to go."

The ceremony was breaking up. Bagpipes marched away from the grave, followed by the Minister and the congregation. Maggie sensed that a man was following close behind, but she didn't feel like looking back.

"Could he still be alive?" Mark said, taking her arm.

"Honey, it was in the papers. That plaque is new . . . an oversight?"

"But could he?"

"Mark."

She loved her son. She had raised him by herself as she struggled to go to college and establish a successful business in New York. She was proud of the man he had become, and she was proud of his wife and of their three small children. When she'd wanted to write her novel, he'd taken over the business, and they'd both succeeded. But he could be exasperating.

"Are his parents still alive? Can we find out?"

"I don't know. Mark, there's just too many bad memories. They never approved of me or my family. They were society. We were servants."

"Did they know about me?"

"No. When Mrs. Langdon called, I didn't know I was pregnant. Then, I became afraid that if they believed you were his son, they would try to take you away. Families did that around here, back then."

"So then, my father wouldn't have known about me either."

"No. But Mark, there's no reason to believe that he's still alive."

"His name's not on that plaque."

"Jesus, Mark! You're exasperating as hell! He's not. Let's not go through any more of this misery." She found her voice rising. "I'm sorry. Look, if he were alive, Mark, he's married with kids of his own. What difference does it make now?"

"Because I want to know and because you've never been able to let him go," Mark said gently.

The crowd pushed from behind harder than before, then someone bumped into Maggie's back.

"Maggie?" The sound came from directly behind her, right into her ear. "God, Maggie?"

Maggie swirled and found herself staring into the blue eyes of Richard Langdon.

Astonished, she choked up, unable to speak. Richard grabbed her and held on for dear life, like she was the last breath that he would ever take.

"God, Maggie, I thought you were dead."

Richard was still handsome although now his face was care-worn, as though plagued with untold unhappiness.

"Your mom told me you were dead. I thought you were—we all thought you were . . ."

"So did I, when I was left for dead, in the jungles of Vietnam." His breaths came in gasps as thought trying to get in a lifetime of misery.

"When they finally found me, my mother had already told you that I was dead. Instead of telling you the truth, she told me you were dead. She would have done anything to destroy our relationship. Father used his influence to get me transferred to Germany. He didn't think I'd stay abroad. The only reason I know you're alive now is because of your book. I rushed home and found out your father died. I thought I'd see you at his funeral."

He stared at Mark.

She said gently, "Richard, this is your son, Mark."

They walked, side by side, following the crowd. Maggie said, "Today, I'm with the most important heroes in my life. My father, my son, and my . . ."

"Husband," Richard said.

The blood rushed to Maggie's head, and she fell against Richard. "Husband?" she asked.

"We're married? I didn't think it was legal."

"Wait . . ." Mark said. "You're *married?*"

"Yes, secretly," Maggie said. "I didn't think it was legal."

"Yes, it was," Richard said, stopping and looking at his son. "You're the spitting image of your mother . . . but, you have my eyes." He grinned. "And my nose. Yes, you do. You look like both of us."

"Damn!" Mark said.

Maggie touched Richard's arm. "Are your parents still alive?" She asked.

Mark shook his head. "No. They passed a few years back. I'm sorry. There's a few things I'd liked to have said to them."

"A lifetime of things," Maggie said. "But that's all behind us now. I hope you haven't gotten married or anything." Her eyebrows scrunched together—a worried look coming over her.

"No . . . No. I hope you're the only family I'll ever want or need. My folks were all shaken up when I refused to marry someone they wanted for me. I told them I'd never marry anyone now that you were gone. I guess it's called Karma." He chuckled and grabbed her around her waist. "We're married. Why don't we stay that way?"

"You mean, I'm really going to have a father? Mom refused to marry any of the men who asked her. And," he added with a sly grin, "there were many."

A wide grin crossed over Richard's face. "There were, were there?"

Maggie raised her eyebrows at him and said, "I could never have married anyone else. I loved you—*love* you. How could I marry anyone else?"

"How indeed?" Richard said. He kissed her.

"Well, I'm going to go find your daughter-in-law and your grand-kids." He turned on his heels and let his mom and dad continue kissing.

Maggie thought this might be a very interesting evening.

The Opera Singer

An opera singer sings her last performance.

Sonia stood in the wings looking over the vast stage and listening to the orchestra warming up in the pit. She looked down at her violet costume that trailed the ground and looked into the mirror that she found next to the lighting panel. Sonia looked like 19th-century elegance with the mixture of violet satin and the black overlay of lace that hung down from her tiny waist. Her shoulders appeared a mixture of peaches and cream in contrast to the dark and rich materials that she wore, and her black wigs of spiral curls balanced the picture. Her appearance startled and fascinated her.

Who was she again? Oh yes, Violetta. The opera was—what? Oh—*"La Traviata."* Did she know this opera? What were her lines? What was she doing *here?* A cold sweat broke out on her forehead, and a hand touched her bare shoulders.

"Nervous Liebchen?" asked a man whose costume suggested that he had to be her leading tenor.

Startled, she turned and faced a handsome young man. "Yes. I guess so. I can't remember the words to anything." She wondered again, what she was doing there . . . who was this man? He seemed distinctly familiar but . . .

"I always get nervous before I go onstage," he said amiably. Once you go on stage, you'll remember." He smiled at her as though they shared an intimate secret and kissed her on her cheek, holding on to her just a little longer than would a mere acquaintance.

"Your rehearsals were superb." He kissed her other cheek. "That's for luck," he said.

"Oh, God, *why am I here?*" she asked herself, then realized she didn't have an answer.

She heard the audience applaud and somehow knew the conductor was in the pit. With the plaintiff first passages of the overture, a hush filled the auditorium. Sonia felt the tragedy and frivolity of the opera engulf her soul. The waiting was interminable, filling her with ecstasy and dread. Then, all it once, it was over. With a mixture of soloists and choristers, she swept onto the stage.

"My God, what's my line?" For some reason, it came, and she suddenly became this mysterious and magical young woman, Violetta. It was as though there was no stage, no audience. Her tenor came to her, and they sang their duet speaking of the pleasures of good wine and good times. What was that he was singing? "One happy day I saw you . . ." He sang as though he loved her. Did he? Why couldn't she remember? How would the audience respond to her? Blending in and out, first loud then soft, caressing each other with their voices, their singing filled the hall. The audience sat on the edge of their seats, enthralled.

Then, she was alone. She looked over the vast audience, and thoughts of stars in a lonely, black sky flashed through her mind. She sang about her superficial life, pretended gaiety, and loneliness. Was this her real life or her imaginary life? The music kept flowing out from her deepest insides as the phrases swept out over the auditorium. How could she know this woman so well? "Follie, Follie" "Pauvre la donna," "Joia." She was on fire. Delicate strains of Verdi emerged, blending orchestra and voice in perfect rapport. The audience went crazy.

Each act was a triumph. Emotions ripped Sonia in two, blending vocal art with theatrical. Each movement was perfectly executed, each phrase perfectly supported, projected, and artistically intertwined. Her dying scene was flawless. The audience wept out loud, and the cast was overcome with emotion.

With her dying words, she stood at the footlight and declared, "I feel a new strength, new life coming into me. Oh Joy!" and with that, she crumbled onto center stage. The audience went wild.

Sonia noticed the audience appeared blurry. The next minute, they seemed distant, and each time the faces grew dimmer and more distant. Then she felt a tap on her shoulder. She turned and saw her tenor dressed in white. Why was he in white, and why was she sitting? And why was the ocean only feet away from her?

"Did you fall asleep again, Sonia?" he asked gently. "She used to be a great opera star," said her tenor, sadly, to another worker.

Looking over the ocean that bordered the front yard for the *Sunnydale Ocean Nursing Home,* Sonia vowed that she wouldn't wake up the next time.

Incident in Ring 4

A dog show judge dies while judging an obedience class.

Ten-year-old Robbie Peterson sat on cold metal bleachers, looking down onto many gates and tables that served as dog show rings. The beginning of Spring break produced its typical nearly freezing Ohio weather, and the Stanton City Ice Arena had little to no insulation. The massive coliseum made up the primary section of the Stanton City Civic Center and was the pride of Stanton City. In addition to the hockey games, the stadium also hosted the Silver Cup Figure Skating Championships and the classy dog shows put on by Stanton City Kennel Club. This year the club had the distinctive honor of holding the National

Collie Club Specialty, which attracted dogs from all over the United States and Canada.

He shivered and surveyed the landscape. Metal crates and grooming tables turned packed aisles into a virtual doggie ghetto. He saw hundreds of prize collies being groomed for their famous collie specialty show by handlers wearing coats and gloves. The smell of grooming lotions and beer being squirted on luscious coats mingled with the scents of eggs and overcooked bacon coming from the canteen. He thought he might be sick.

Robbie, bored and cold, huddled against the neck of his favorite best friend, Roxi. Roxi was a tri-color collie, black, tan, and white with a full white collar and white paws. Exuding personality and a certain amount of compassion, she allowed Robbie to warm his face and hands in her fur. At the same time, she tried to crawl up on his lap. Robbie thought that it was going to be a long five days.

His inquisitive deep-blue eyes shifted up to the international flags hanging from the rafters and back down into the arena just below where dogs performed obedience routines. He listened to members of the packed audience behind him, trying to explain the different dog events.

"Now, dear, confirmation is where they judge the dog on structure and movement as it pertains to the breed standard. Obedience is, well, all that is, is the dog's ability to perform certain basic commands and routines in the ring."

Robbie turned and looked at the pair—a prim mother on the stout side and her sour-faced daughter wearing matching collie sweatshirt, collie jackets, and matching caps.

"All that is," he mimicked in his mind. God, it took months, if not years, to teach some of those routines. He turned his head back to the ring where twelve dogs lined in the Obedience Ring to do their group exercises. The imposing figure of the Judge, Tyrone Bartholomew Scott, directed twelve handlers to "sit" their dogs. He was a tall, handsome man standing, proud, straight, and, Robbie thought, just a bit formidable. Robbie remembered hearing tales of his scandalous divorce two years ago and smiled to himself. His Mom wouldn't be pleased, he recalled.

Mr. Scott commanded, "Sit your dogs," and the handlers said "sit" in unison. Mr. Scott said, "Leave your dogs." The response never followed, for just then, he toppled over and crashed onto the floor. As though directed by a conductor's baton, the massive crowd hushed, and all movement came to a halt.

Stunned, Robbie suddenly became one with the packed stadium full of spectators. Everything seemed to move in slow—or no—motion at all, and when he finally realized he had to breathe, he gasped for air. He moved out of the bleachers and down the stairs to the main floor. Running around and through the crowds, Robbie reached Ring Four in time to run into his dad's friend, Dr. Kenneth Novak, standing outside the ring with his dog.

"Robbie, hold him, okay?" Dr. Novak said, more as a command than a request. Accompanying a ring steward, he entered the ring with Robbie and the two dogs trailing behind.

"Oh, Wow!" Robbie said, wanting to be unnoticed but not succeeding.

"Come on, son, this isn't the place for you." The ring steward said. He took Doctor Novak's dog and escorted Robbie and Roxi out of the ring. The crowd parted like the Red Sea as security and officials hurried their way through the coliseum. Once outside, Robbie turned around and inched his way back. Ken Novak leaned over him and shook his head to tell everyone what Robbie already knew—the judge was dead.

Robbie heard bits and snatches of the officials' conversation.

"I don't like this," Dr. Novak said, scrutinizing the dead man and shaking his head.

"Heart attack?"

"Could be." He looked up at the official and raised one dark-brown eyebrow.

"What do you mean, could be?"

"It probably was. Er—we need to get the body moved."

"Oh, *no*!" A blond-haired woman of about forty rushed over to the group and looked down at the body. She knelt down and touched the dead man's face. "Oh, no. Not him!"

"Willie, this is no place for you." George Billhof, an official with a distinguished head of steely, grey hair and icy blue eyes, bent over and lifted her to her feet.

"Oh, no, George. What happened?" She looked at George. "Is he . . . ?"

"Yes, I'm afraid so." George put his arm around Wilhelmina Crabbit.

"Not again. Not so soon after . . ."

"Ambulance here—" Another official appeared in the ring.

Robbie watched as two ambulance attendants carried a stretcher into the ring and carried the body out, followed by Ken, George, Willie, and the ring stewards. Robbie looked around at the confusion and sighed. It was the most bizarre thing he had seen at a dog show—since the time his mom and dad had gotten into that knockdown, drag-out fight a couple of months ago that led to their pending divorce. The crowd mulled around the coliseum, shocked but now talking about the incident and shaking their heads. They waited, not knowing whether the show would continue.

"Robbie!" His mother ran up into the confusion and grabbed her son, while George Billhof grabbed her.

"Laura," said George frantically. "We've got to get a new judge."

Laura and Robbie sat in George Billhof's office while Max Calhoun, the American Kennel Club Representative, loomed over him. George contemplated doubling up the assignment, but the show was already *so* big—maybe—Alan would be available. He picked up the phone and dialed.

"Alan? I'm *so* glad to find you home. Thought you were judging in Canada this weekend. Oh? That's next week. Great! Listen. I need a favor.

Tyrone Scott—know him? Our obedience judge just dropped dead in the ring. We're desperate. What? Oh, of a heart attack, I think. You will? Thanks, Alan, I owe you." He breathed a sigh of relief as he put down the receiver and looked at the expectant faces.

"He'll do it. He'll be here in ten minutes" George walked out and announced the show would continue despite a slight delay to wait for the replacement judge.

Alan Peterson came into the room accompanied by Ken Novak, who waived onlookers away.

"Dad!" Robbie shouted.

"Robbie!" shouted his dad grinning from ear to ear despite the tension around him.

"Did you hear about the judge? Huh, Dad?"

"Your father's here to replace him," George Billhof said.

"Alan!" Ken Novak came out of a room where he'd examined the body and tapped him on the shoulder. "Would you come over here a moment?"

"What? What's wrong? Haven't they taken him out of here yet?" Alan asked, walking over to Ken and peering into one of the adjoining rooms that had served as Stanton City's Kennel Club's business office and training facility for the past five years. George cast a disparaging glance at the doctor but kept quiet.

"Alan is the retired Chief-Of-Police in Stanton. We could use his help," Dr. Novak replied to George's sour expression.

"Oh, Great!" George was seething. "I brought him here to *judge.*"

"What's the problem, Ken?" Alan asked.

Ken whispered in Alan's ear. Robbie and George strained to hear what they said, but Alan's voice was too soft.

"I think we need to go into the office." Alan's voice turned into his official police chief tone.

Robbie followed them. For his ten-year-old imagination, this was much more interesting than the show ring. Jeez! Robbie caught his breath. The show ring! Would he miss his class? He decided that he hoped so as he watched his father say hello to the man who had been his Dad's partner and now was the new chief of police.

"Danny!" Alan greeted Daniel Summers.

"Great to see you, Chief."

"Nah, *you're* the Chief now. But, what's this all about?"

"Yeah," George said, "Who called you? Tyrone Scott died of a heart attack. Uh . . . Here, sit down." George sat behind his desk. The others plunked down onto leather chairs grouped with a matching sofa and surrounding a coffee table made of driftwood and glass housing recent issues of the *Collie Club Annual* and *The American Kennel Club Gazette*.

Original portraits of famous collies hung on the walls. Between them, photos of George Billhof, Wilhelmina Crabbit, and Tyrone Bartholomew Scott resting in a silver frame, holding a champion collie and a winners' trophy—a sterling silver cup.

Alan studied the photos and paintings around the room.

Bet there's a lot of money in this room—money, yes, but also an enormous ego.

"I called," the doctor said. "As luck would have it, Chief Summers was in his office. I thought it wouldn't hurt. He's just down the hall and around the corner, and . . . there's something I don't like."

"What?" asked Alan and Danny simultaneously. "What?" Robbie, in his excitement, nearly stomped on Roxi's paw. She yelped and jumped back.

"Oh, sorry, Roxi."

"Well, I don't like . . . It appears like a heart attack and, maybe it was. On the other hand, it could be an overdose of something which induced an attack. Did Tyrone do drugs?"

"*Drugs?*" George was incredulous. "I sincerely doubt it, Ken."

"Overdose? Drugs?" Alan's eyes grew wide. "Tyrone Bartholomew Scott?"

"Mr. Scott was squeaky clean," George said, "and he made sure everyone else was too."

"I don't know for sure, just suspect. I was talking to Tyrone before he went into the ring . . . he seemed confused . . . saw haloes around the light. He mentioned everyone looking like angels or something. When he found the ring, he couldn't decide where he wanted anything. First, he wanted his table in one spot and then in another. Then he kept changing his mind about his performance patterns. Couldn't decide what he wanted his handlers to do—go fast or slow, which jump to take, sit or . . . Scott is one of the most organized judges in the business. Not like him at all.

"I'm ordering an autopsy and blood analysis. If I hadn't seen him and spoke to him, I'd have signed the death certificate right away. Anyway, as I said, we'll see."

You suspect some kind of drug, then? I can't believe that Tyrone took hallucinogens

Was it LSD?" Alan looked over at his son and wondered if he should be there.

"Wow!" Robbie's eyes bugged out of his head just as a knock was heard at the door.

"Robbie!" A tall, slender woman with auburn hair entered the room, green eyes fixed on her son. "I've been frantic with worry when you didn't show up at the ring." She stopped when she saw Alan's presence in the room.

"Alan! What are *you* doing here?" She stared across the room at him for a minute, then involuntarily, she bit her bottom lip. Alan thought she looked ill-at-ease.

"George asked me to be the replacement judge for Scott," he replied. "Robbie came up to say hello. Sorry about his disappearance. He's been here." The tone of his voice came out, "It's my fault." *I blew it again.* He was angry at himself.

"You made Robbie miss his class."

"Er—Mrs. Peterson, Laura," George said, breaking the tension. "We have an investigation going on here. Do you mind if we continue?"

"Investigation? About what? I thought it was a heart attack."

"Mom! Mr. Scott died of an *overdose of drugs!*"

"What?" Relaxing her body, Laura flashed a look at her husband. "You're letting a ten-year-old boy . . . Of all the irresponsible . . ." Laura stammered, not able to find the right words. She grabbed Robbie and dragged him out of the room, Roxi trailing along behind.

"Sorry, Alan," Danny said with sympathy. He'd been through his own piece of domestic hell when he'd been divorced by his first wife. The life of a cop was never easy. Both Danny and Al's marriages had been casualties of a law enforcement lifestyle. Even Alan's retiring from the force couldn't patch the riff, which cracked his marriage. The dog shows had fractured the crack creating the remaining major fissure.

"Alan," Danny said, "we have a problem here. Ken thinks that it might not have been a heart attack."

"Well, not quite." All eyes focused on Doctor Ken Novak. "I think he was on something, or someone might have given him something."

"God! That means that someone might have deliberately *murdered* him," Alan said.

Doctor Novak slowly nodded his head. "I'm going to ask for a blood work-up."

"How long will that take?" Danny asked.

"Normally, if a full battery of tests is requested, it wouldn't be back for about 3-5 days. The hospital normally sends the tests out to the pharmaceutical companies. I will request a rush and ask for some specific tests they normally don't do. If they can do it right there, I should have at least some indication by later today. Meanwhile, I suggest that you act as though it was a heart attack, okay?"

"Meanwhile," said George, shuffling in his seat, "We need you in the obedience ring, okay?"

The day crept by slowly. Alan worked in the obedience ring, trying to keep everything upbeat—not an easy job. The exhibitors were overcome with shock and apprehension. Robbie missed his first class but managed to make it into the obedience class in the afternoon. He blew it because he was watching his father judge in the other ring.

Laura Peterson's face filled with tension. She watched her son watch his father as he tried to show his dog. *He misses him. So do I. What went wrong? Why a divorce—it's too painful.* Their marriage splintered because of his life on the police force. *But he's no longer on the force.*

But then, there were the dogs. They raised their collies—showed them—promoted them. But gradually, Alan slipped into "that other sport—obedience." By the time he retired from the force, their ability to get along was an all-time low. But this—this was worse. She wondered if depriving Robbie of his dad was the best thing. It was Alan that wanted the divorce, wasn't it?

"He overdosed on a prescription of Digitalis. That's a medication used for people with heart problems." Late Friday night, Ken and Alan sat in Danny's office in the Police Department area of the Civic Center. The room was large, a duplicate of George's office on the other side of the complex. It accommodated an area with chairs and a sofa, ready for interviews and meetings. The color scheme of maroon and grey was designed to calm the frantic clients that he sometimes interviewed.

"Did Mr. Scott have heart problems?"

"I think that Lucinda, that's his ex-wife, told me he did," George said.

"Oh?" asked Ken in bewilderment.

"Why? What would be strange about digitalis being given to a heart patient?" Alan asked.

Everyone looked at Ken.

"Because he was also on a thyroid hormone, that's why. The two are deadly when taken together."

"Who told you that?" George asked.

"Lucinda said he'd been on thyroid hormones for several years."

"Kill him? You mean murder? Someone murdered Tyrone Bartholomew Scott?" George grilled Ken, looking intensely into his face.

"So, who would want to kill him?" Danny asked, shaking his head.

"Maybe quite a few people," George said.

Alan ignored George's comment, blew away a lock of his blond hair from in front of one watchful eye.

"You know—er, *knew* him?" Danny asked, picking up a pencil lying on his desk.

"A little—by reputation mostly," Alan said. "We judged together at a few shows."

"Murder at a dog show. Good title for a mystery. You think an irate exhibitor?" Danny began to tap the pencil on his desk.

"Possibly, but probably not," Alan said. "That just doesn't happen. More likely, they'll get even with him next time *he's* in the ring. If it was an exhibitor, there must have been another motive. Who was with him before he went into the ring?"

"Well, for one, I was," Ken said. "That's why I thought it was more than a heart attack. He complained of eye problems—said everyone looked like angels. There were haloes around the lights. He was disoriented. I had to point him to the right ring.

"Nothing his ring stewards did for him was right. First, he wanted his table in one spot and then changed it back again. Then the mats were wrong.

"My first impression when he mentioned the haloes was Glaucoma. My second was that he was on something. But I was getting ready to show my dog, so I didn't think much more about it until he fell over in the ring."

George said, "When he arrived at the show, I took him to the cafeteria. The show committee—I'm head of that—provides breakfast and lunch for the judges and the staff."

"Who else was there?" Alan asked. He looked over at Danny. "Sorry, Dan. It's your investigation."

"Not at all. I'm grateful for your help. Go ahead."

"Well, let's see . . ." George stared at the ceiling, apparently thinking. "There was a judge from conformation, Mrs. Crabbit, Willie er Wilhelmina Crabbit. She judges the rough collies, er that's the long-haired dogs . . ." he said for the benefit of Danny, who just shrugged his shoulders.

"I know that." He blew out an irritated sigh.

"Did she know Scott?" Alan asked, trying to diffuse the situation. Dan didn't like being corrected.

"They all know each other, Alan. You should know that," George said irritably. "Or, at least most of them know each other."

"Hm, yes. I guess we all do know each other, more or less. Mrs. Crabbit sat next to Tyrone, and I sat at the table's head—but only for a few minutes. I left them together. I had other things to attend to back here. Oh, Lucinda Scott. She's judging the smooths—the ones with very little coat . . ." he said again. Allan thought this was once again for the benefit of Danny. "And sat across from them next to the other obedience judge, Norman Webster."

Danny raised an eyebrow then his smile became a grimace. "I know the difference between a smooth collie and a rough collie. I used to show collies, myself, remember?"

"Hmm. Yes, I remember. Anyway, I don't think Norman knows anyone, though. He's from California. This is his first assignment in the Midwest. Anyway, Lucinda gave me an earful at lunch."

"What did she say?" Alan encouraged him.

"Well, she said that Tyrone had a heart condition."

"Since when?"

"Don't know," George replied, "Just repeating what Lucinda said. Didn't know it wasn't natural. I just shook my head in sympathy."

Danny turned to George. "Did she get along with her ex?"

"Oh, I suppose as well as any divorced couple," he replied carefully. "Why?"

"Would she have a reason to want to kill her husband—er, ex-husband?"

"Perhaps. Scott, I believe, was interested in another woman. He mentioned it to me on the way from the airport. He was excited because he would be judging with her."

"Who was the lady?" Alan asked. "Oh, you mean . . ."

"Yes, Willie—er, Mrs. Crabbit."

"Is she married now?" Danny got up and sat on his desk. He looked down on Alan and George.

George flushed.

"Widowed. Still—he was interested in other women. There was, for instance, your ex." He looked at Alan.

"Laura?" Alan was astonished.

"Oh, don't worry. I don't think Laura was interested in him. Although I don't believe that Lucinda knew that. She thought Tyrone would go after Mrs. Peterson now that she was getting a divorce. Sorry, Alan. It's what she thought."

"Actually, he was really interested in where the money was. Mrs. Crabbit is the heir to the Crabbit fortune."

"You mean Crabbit Fixtures? *That* Crabbit?"

"Yes, that's the family. Her husband was a self-made man."

"When did he die?" Alan asked almost nonchalantly, his eyes, however, locked onto George's features seeking information. His cop mode was back in full force.

"Last year, in a boating accident."

"Oh, how?" Alan pumped with his voice.

"Sail-boating. He was messing with the sail, and an unexpected wind change knocked the beam into his head and sent him flying overboard. He was dead before we could get to him."

"You were there?" Now fidgeting, Danny slid off his desk and returned to his chair.

"Yes."

Danny looked at George tapping his pencil on his desk. Alan remembered that Danny always tapped his pencil on his desk when he was preoccupied.

"So—who was there this morning?" Danny continued to tap. Annoyed, Alan shook his head at him. The tapping stopped.

"Uh, Chief, we've been over this already," George replied.

"This morning isn't relative," Dr. Novak said suddenly. "What killed T.B. Scott was administered last night." All three men turned to look at him.

"This stuff takes at least eight hours to react."

"So, now George, who was at dinner with Mr. Scott last night?" Danny now tapping more rapidly with his pencil.

"Well, I met Laura and Robbie at the Sheraton, then Mrs. Crabbit came in with Mr. Scott."

"They came in together?" Danny asked.

"Laura and Robbie were already in the lobby, waiting. I drove Tyrone Scott from the airport, and Willie pulled up behind us in a separate car. We just happened to arrive at the same time. Then, we all went into the dining room and had a cocktail before we ordered dinner. In the middle, I remember, the waiter had just brought in our drinks, Lucinda came in . . ."

Just then, Robbie and Laura entered the room.

"Oh," she said, "Excuse me. You wanted to see me?"

Alan went over and pushed a chair up for her between George's chair and Danny's desk. Robbie sat on a window seat next to his dad.

"We're just trying to get some movements from last night," Danny said, trying to look official but looking uncomfortable in the presence of his friends.

George continued. "Like I was saying, the waiter brought our drinks."

"What did everyone order?" Alan asked.

"Why?" Laura looked at her husband with curiosity.

George answered the question. "I ordered my usual Seven and Seven. Willie had a Whiskey Sour, Tyrone Scott had a Gin and Tonic, I think. Yes, that's it."

"I had a Gin and Tonic, and Robbie had a coke," Laura said firmly. "But why these questions? What's going on?"

"Laura," Alan said as gently as he could, "We think Tyrone might have been murdered."

"Oh! Oh no!"

"Wow!" Robbie said, his eyes bugging out and his face lighting up like a Christmas tree.

"Robbie, quiet," his father said, a stern tone coming into his voice.

"Just as we started to toast, we were interrupted by Lucinda, who came in rather out of breath. She flew in from Miami and took a cab from the airport. She must have taken an earlier flight because she wasn't scheduled to come in until later. Anyway, she ordered, and we drank to each other's health. After that, Pamela Wyatt, President of the Stanton Kennel Club, sat with us. She didn't eat."

"How come?"

"She ate with her family. Her husband's pretty sticky about that. Not a dog person, but that's another story."

"What's her relationship to Scott?" asked Danny.

Laura piped in, "I don't think that Pamela knew him. She hired him on my recommendation."

"Why did you recommend him?"

Alan eyed Laura curiously. Was she—*could* she have been involved with that pompous twit?

"Because he's a good judge. That's why," she replied. She looked over at her husband as though reading his mind. "He's hard, but he's fair. Also, there wasn't anyone else from this immediate vicinity that was available."

"Alan was . . ." George replied, not too tactfully. Laura looked down at the floor, and George stopped speaking.

"I can't blame her for that, George. That's very understandable, under the circumstances," Alan said. Laura looked at him gratefully.

"Still . . ." Danny said slowly. "Was there something between you and Mr. Scott?"

"Certainly not!" Laura was hot. "Where did you ever get such an idea?"

Robbie's eyes grew wide to his mother's anger. Danny didn't reply—watching Alan's face, which remained deadpan.

"What happened during dinner?" Alan focused back on the investigation. Soon after their arrival, the waiters brought cocktails. Lucinda came in late. Conversation and well wishes were exchanged, and dinner was served. The only interesting thing happened when Lucinda's hand accidentally knocked over Laura's drink and had to be replaced.

Dogs were discussed, and events of the next day were addressed. Robbie looked bored just listening to the rehash of Tuesday night's dinner conversation.

"Robbie?" Alan's gaze fixed back on Robbie as he stared out into space. He wished he had the luxury of being in a ten-year-old's world sometimes.

"I think it's time that we went home . . . if you don't need me anymore?" Laura asked.

"No, if we need you, we'll find you tomorrow at the show."

Laura smiled. "Well, at least you won't have far to travel for this case, Chief. However, I'd appreciate it if you'd wait until after the show. It is the last day, you know," she said, straightening her green silk blouse, which had started to come out of her beige jeans. "We really have enough to do." Alan grinned despite what was going on. His wife's blouse matched her eyes.

"Oh!" Robbie said as though remembering something. "Mr. Summers? About Tuesday night."

"What about Tuesday night, son?" Alan asked.

"Robbie, come *on!*" his mother called. She was now halfway out the door. Robbie looked at the men looking at him.

"What about Tuesday night, Robbie?" George prompted.

Robbie shook his head. "Oh, nothing, I guess. Never mind. I guess I just wasn't paying attention. Bye, Dad." Robbie, once again, did the unexpected. He flung his arms around his dad's neck and ran out of the room.

"Laura and Tyrone had the same thing to drink," Ken said, a funny tone coming into his voice.

"Yeah, so?" George asked.

"It was Lucinda's hand that knocked over her drink?" Ken asked George.

"Yes. I already told you that. Why?"

"There were three women in there who were involved with this guy?"

"Laura said she *wasn't*," Alan said, his face turning red.

"Yeah, but did anyone other than Laura know that?"

"What are you getting at?" Alan asked.

"I don't know. It doesn't make sense." Danny kept tapping his pencil now more rapidly.

"Danny, would you knock off the tapping?"

"Oh, sorry . . . Alan, do you know anyone who might have it in for Laura?" Danny asked, standing up and towering over the two men.

"Laura? To incriminate her?"

"No, Alan. I mean, kill her."

Alan's stood, and his face turned white. "Kill her? Christ, there were only seven people there, including you, George, Laura, Robbie and Tyrone, himself. Why would anyone want to kill Laura?" Alan shook his head.

Danny motioned for Alan to sit, and Alan sat.

"You mean it was meant for Laura?" George asked.

"Who could get their hands on Digitalis? And give it to Laura?"

"Well, any one of them, I would think," George said. "Willie's husband had heart problems, and he was on the medication. Lucinda's father was recently hospitalized from a heart attack, and she's been caring for him. I just visited them recently. He was in a wheelchair."

"And you're a Pharmacist, aren't you, George?"

"Why would I want to kill the best show organizer I ever had? That's stupid," George said, disgust creeping into his voice.

"Laura? Somehow I can't picture anyone hating Laura enough to want to kill her," Alan said. "Maybe Tyrone was the intended victim all the time."

"Hm, maybe. Tyrone was rich. Their divorce made the papers, I remember. It was on the society pages for a month. Lucinda, I remember, wasn't happy about the split up. They had a major battle for custody of the dogs, I think," George said. "I know Lucinda was surprised at seeing his name on the roster. She wasn't sure she wanted the assignment. Then, she decided to do it anyway. There was a rumor that he was engaged to someone. As I said, I think it was Willie, but I'm not sure the others knew that." George got up and nodded to Alan and Danny. "Gentlemen, it's getting late. I'd better be going. Good night."

As the dog show progressed the next day, bits and snatches of thinly disguised interviews could be heard.

"Mrs. Scott, I'm so sorry about your ex-husband. Were you two still friendly? I heard that there was a major battle when he divorced you?" Lucinda looked at Danny Summers as she started to enter her ring. She stopped and turned toward him, a piece of her exquisitely coiffed red hair falling out of a tortoiseshell clip. A sour expression came onto her face.

"She could do anything she set her mind to and pull it off." he thought. Then, he waited for her reply.

"Mr. Policeman," Lucinda said with a snort, "Despite all the newspaper reports that you may have heard, Tyrone did *not* divorce me. I divorce *him* for philandering. He, sir, was a womanizer. I did not kill my ex-husband, Mr. Summers. And, yes, we were still friendly. We liked each other. We just couldn't get along. Now, if you'll excuse me . . ." She turned her back to Danny and entered her ring to judge the waiting smooth collies gathered around.

Alan watched as Willie Crabbit picked out the "Best of American Bred Collie" class winner at Ring One. Alan approved. He would have picked the same dog.

"Hi, Willie!" he called as she came out of the ring.

"Alan! How nice to see you!" Willie always looked like she was glad to see everyone who spoke to her. It was her way, her *charm*. It was evident, however, that Tyrone's death had taken its toll. Her eyes were bloodshot, and her expression was one of profound sorrow.

"Can we talk?"

"Sure, I have a few minutes," she said, as she brushed a lock of hair back behind her ear. Wilhelmina always looked like a million dollars, and it wasn't just the money. This woman, he thought, would ooze with class even if she bought her clothes s at a second-hand Salvation Army store. It was her personality, and he liked it. He grinned at her.

"I'm helping in the investigation of Tyrone's death, Willie. You know, the police suspect that he was murdered, don't you?"

"Yes. Yes, I heard. We were told this morning," Lucinda said, a deep sorrow in her voice. Then looking up at him and smiling despite moist eyes, she said, "Who better? I'll tell you anything you want to know."

"Thanks, Willie. There's been a rumor that you were engaged to him?"

"Well, now, I'd say engaged was an exaggeration. We saw an enormous amount of each other, though. Tyrone was an old devil, a man who loved women. Despite that, I cared about him. I'm going to miss him." The smile seemed to vanish, and a haunted look replaced it. "It was the second time in a year that I lost someone I loved."

"I'm sorry, Willie. I really am. Did you drive up with him?"

"No, not with him. But, we happened to arrive at the same time, Tuesday night."

"Did you notice anything unusual at dinner?"

"No. Except, Lucinda came in late, and she knocked over someone's drink. I think it was Laura's."

"Did you see it?"

"No. George came to her rescue and helped clean up the mess. Then, he ordered another drink for her."

"What did Tyrone do?"

"He was busy greeting Lucinda and being gallant to Laura."

"Dad!" Robbie came running up with his dog, who jumped up on Alan. Then Willie's dog, Boo, jumped on Willie putting his paws on her shoulder, and licked her face. At last, he sat on Robbie's foot and scratched behind his ear. Willie laughed.

"Dad, I need to talk to you."

"Not now, Robbie," said his mother catching up to him. "You're going into the Junior Showmanship ring. You're getting ready now. *March!*"

"Aw, Mom!" Laura ushered Robbie back toward his ring.

"You have a wonderful boy there," Willie sighed. "I wish—oh, how I wish—but, oh well, no regrets. I guess we had money instead."

"I have a very delicate question I need to ask you," Alan said. "Do you think Tyrone wanted to marry you because of your money?"

"You may well ask!" she replied. "No, I don't think so. Tyrone has plenty of money of his own . . . er, had. He didn't need mine. After my husband died, Tyrone and George were both very kind to me. I guess I might have hurt George's feelings. I think he was interested in a relationship, but Tyrone and I got closer. Anyway, no, I don't believe Tyrone was after my money. If it were George, now—well, that's . . . Oops! I've got to go. More dogs. Excellent selection this year! Here I come!" She called, waving to her ring steward.

"Wait, only one more question, Willie. This is important." Willie stopped and walked back. "Yes?"

"Did you hear anything about Tyrone being involved with Laura?"

"Laura?" Willie was astonished, then she laughed out loud. "Balderdash! Tyrone flirted with everyone. Don't even let that enter your head." She started to turn back to her ring then changed her mind. "Alan, it's none of my business, but—I've never let that stop me yet. Laura is a good—good person, and your son is the best. Don't let them get away. Life is way too short." She smiled a rather sad smile and went back into her ring.

George and Willie and Tyrone and Willie's husband—How did that enter into the picture? In the picture on the credenza, the woman was Willie Crabbit. What about Laura? Who had told him about Tyrone's being interest in Laura? And who said that Tyrone had heart problems? Who provided all that information about . . . ? Alan tried to piece everything together. Something nagged in the back of his mind. What he'd been told somehow wasn't gelling with something. He wasn't sure what. Alan's head began to hurt, and exhibitors and dogs bumped into him as he stood still, staring amongst an ocean of people and dogs in the middle of the aisle. Then he thought about his son. What did Robbie want to tell him?

"*Oh, shit!*" Suddenly, he pulled himself together and ran, bumping and elbowing people out of the way, over to the ring where the kids were getting ready to show their dogs.

"Laura, where's Robbie?"

"Getting ready for his class, Alan. Can't you wait until he's finished?"

"No, Laura, I'm not sure it can wait." He did the unexpected, once more, and put his arms around his wife and kissed her.

"What the . . . ?"

"Laura, the class is going in . . ." A ring steward called to her. Kids were milling around, and parents were giving last-minute instructions.

"Now dear, remember, always watch your judge. Do exactly what he tells you to do."

Robbie and Roxi weren't there.

"Oh, No! Not again. Alan, this is your fault," Laura said, an accusing tone in her voice.

"No. No, it's not. I don't know where Robbie is, Laura, but I'm afraid. He wanted to talk to me about something last night and again just now. Laura, I think he saw something Tuesday night."

"Hi, Petersons!" Danny came strolling up to them.

"Danny, have you seen Robbie?" Alan asked.

"No! Isn't he with you? I thought he was supposed to show his dog."

"He is!" Laura said.

"Where's George?" Alan asked. He kept looking around-not able to focus on Laura or Danny.

"Don't know. I guess he's doing Show Secretary stuff."

"Danny, come on!" Alan yelled over the mass of voices coming from all sides.

Robbie suited up and gave his dog a last-minute going over as George approached.

"Robbie, son, your father wants to talk to you about what you saw Tuesday night."

"But, Mr. Billhof, I have to go into the ring. My mom will kill me!"

"You still have time. Your Dad and Mr. Summers are in my office. You can bring Roxi along and then go back to the ring. Come on!"

Robbie followed George into his office.

"Where's Dad?"

"Don't know—said he'd meet us here. Maybe he got tied up talking to someone," George said, turning his back on Robbie and fiddling with something in his credenza drawer. A low throaty growl came from Roxi.

"Roxi—stop!" Robbie said and didn't notice George walking over to the door and turn the lock.

"Now, son, what was it that you saw last night?" he said, going back over to the credenza and pulling something out of the drawer. Another low-throated growl came from the dog. This time it had a sharper ring.

"Roxi—stop! I don't know why he's acting that way, Mr. Billhof," Robbie said, starting to realize precisely why Roxi was acting that way.

"Robbie! Answer the question." George's voice demanded.

"No, I didn't see anything." Robbie protested.

"Yes—yes, you did. What was it?"

Robbie needed to stall for time. He looked over at the door leading to the outside.

George said, "Son, you can't get out that way. It's locked—inside and out. Now, Robbie, what did you see Tuesday night?"

"Uh, yeah. I saw *you!* I saw you knock that drink over," Robbie said.

Robbie noticed Roxi's hair stand up on end, but George seemed not to notice—or care—as he stood with a piece of cotton in his hand.

"What else, son?" asked George inching his way over to Robbie—and keeping one eye on the Collie's bared teeth.

"You put something into Mr. Scott's drink. I didn't notice at the time." Robbie frantically searched for something to say as he tried to figure out how to get out of the situation.

"Grrr," Roxi growled, inching her way forward, crawling on all fours.

"Call her off, son," George's voice was quiet and threatening.

"Uh, Rox . . ." A knock was heard at the door.

"Ssh—" George said.

"Robbie!" It was Laura.

"*Mom!*" Robbie screamed, and several things happened at once.

George moved toward Robbie, and Roxi moved toward George as the pounding at the door got louder.

Roxi lunged.

George met the dog's muzzle with his palm, and the dog fell to the ground.

"Roxi! No!" Robbie screamed again. George grabbed the kid and put the cotton up toward Robbie's nose.

"Don't even think about it!" A voice said outside the window. A shot blasted from the inside door, and Danny, Laura, Lucinda, and Willie all tumbled into the room. As George turned, Alan crashed through the window.

"Drop it!" Alan ordered.

George dropped the chloroformed cotton ball.

Robbie ran to Roxi as Danny cuffed George and read him his rights. George seemed to lose control and lunged at two police officers when they tried to lead him out of the room, nearly knocking Laura over a chair.

Alan went over and put his hand on Roxi's head as she lay still. "She'll be okay, Robbie. She's just been stunned," he said as Robbie laid his head over Roxi's and softly started to cry.

"How did you know?" Laura asked.

They all sat in George's office, stunned after the police hauled George out of the room. They looked at Alan, who was rubbing his sore shoulder and picking glass out of his shirt.

"You okay?" Laura asked.

"Yeah, just bruised. Don't think I hit any arteries or anything."

"So, how did you know?" she persisted.

"I just pieced a couple of things together," he said, trying to remember everything. "First, I remembered how surprised Lucinda was that Tyrone was judging."

"Yes, I was. Everyone thought it was because Tyrone was my ex-husband, and I hated him. Not true. Actually, we got along pretty well. We just couldn't be married to each other. No, the reason was because Tyrone was responsible for George's ouster from the AKC judging panel. He caught George fixing a class."

Pamela Wyatt stood at the doorway, listening to the proceedings. When Lucinda had caught her breath, she sat down and said, "George never forgave him for that. I was surprised when George let Laura hire him. God! I never thought he'd kill someone over it."

"He didn't," Alan said. "Although it probably intensified his desire. The real reason was a bit more practical. George wanted to marry Willie. Willie threw George over for Tyrone, then inherited millions when her husband died."

"I see . . ." Willie said. Tears trickled down, and Laura put her arm around her.

"It would have come off. The digitalis was coupled with Tyrone's thyroid hormones. He would have dropped dead, and everyone would have thought it was a natural heart attack, except for the sharp eyes of Ken Novak, who just happened to be close to his ring at the time."

"Hi!" Everyone turned. Ken walked into the ring. "Heard you got your man, Chief."

Alan continued, "It would have come off. He knocked over Laura's drink when everyone's attention was elsewhere, and he put the digitalis in Tyrone's Gin and Tonic. The effect wouldn't be obvious for about eight hours. Then when Ken suspected it was intentional, George did everything he could to change our focus. He knew Willie's husband had heart problems and how easy it would be for anyone to get hold of that medication. He steered your relationship away by implicating Lucinda—I suspect that was started by Danny's thoughts that Laura might have been the victim. You played right into his hands Chief."

"I did?"

"Whatever do you mean, next victim, Alan?" Laura asked.

"He mentioned that Tyrone Scott was interested in you. I was almost convinced that Lucinda had put the stuff into your glass and missed and hit Scott by mistake. A large dose of that stuff could kill anyone."

"Oh!" Laura shook her head.

"My word! I'd never do such a thing." Lucinda said. She snorted. "Actually, I knew about Tyrone's involvement with Willie. I thought it was great. If anyone could have kept him at home, it was her."

"Thanks," Willie murmured, still suffering from shock.

"But Robbie saw it, didn't you?" Alan said.

Robbie nodded. "Mrs. Scott didn't knock off Mom's drink."

"I didn't?" Lucinda was incredulous. "I thought my sleeve caught it and knocked it over."

"No. George just wanted it to look that way," Alan replied.

"Oh! Now I remember. He reached for something across the table, and as his arm crossed back, his elbow pushed my hand. It happened so fast!"

"As everyone was trying to help clean up the mess, Mr. Billhof's hand hovered over Mr. Scott's drink," Robbie said.

"Did you actually see him slip something into it?" Danny asked.

"No, just his hand hovering over the glass."

"We have no actual proof?" Willie asked.

"Just his confession," Danny said.

"He confessed?"

"More like cracked up. Tyrone was laughing like a hyena on the way back to the cells. He kept repeating, "I nearly pulled it off . . . I nearly pulled it off. Over and over again. They had to put a straight jacket on the guy."

"He was insane? No! How? Why?" Willie asked, still not comprehending.

"I think he probably had some psychological pathologies. He was an egotist. An egomaniac. He wanted revenge, and—he wanted your money. He thought you'd marry him if Tyrone was out of the way."

"But I'd never have married him. He—well, George was on the deck when my husband went over. I always thought that George could have rescued him. George was a marvelous swimmer."

"He probably could have," said Alan as gently as possible.

"In the back of my mind, I thought, perhaps that he had . . ." Willie didn't finish.

"Pushed him?"

"Well, maybe, I guess we'll never know. My husband had a lump on the back of his head. The coroner attributed his death to a blow on the head from the sail. It could have been something else.

Robbie was on the floor cradling Roxi as Lucinda looked at Willie, Pamela, and Danny, and said, "Don't we have a dog show to run?"

"Yes, let's go back to our rings. Lunch break's over." Willie said.

"What lunch?" Lucinda asked.

"Oh, Mr. Summers, why don't you come too?" Willie said to Danny with her head nodding toward Laura, Alan, and Robbie.

"Oh! Oh, yeah! I have a bit of paperwork to do." They all streamed out of the splintered door, leaving the Petersons alone.

"Robbie, she'll be all right," Alan said, slipping off the chair and onto the floor next to his son. Laura found herself on the floor next to Alan.

"Look, Laura. Can't we . . . ?" Alan stopped, and Robbie looked at him. "What split us up? I can't even remember," he added thoughtfully.

"It had to do with the dogs. It was you and your obedience ring versus me and my involvement with the conformation ring. We couldn't get along, and Robbie . . ."

"Isn't that a little dumb on our part? And can't Robbie make up his own mind? Maybe he'd rather just throw sticks and go swimming with Roxi in the pond."

"It wasn't only that," Laura replied slowly. "It stemmed from your life as a cop. I lived in mortal fear that one day you wouldn't come back. It wasn't just the dogs. We were at odds about everything."

"Laura, if you didn't love me, you wouldn't have been so afraid of my not coming home. Don't you realize that?" Alan got up and walked over to the window, not wanting to confront her expression. "Look." He said, turning back towards her. "How many families do you know that have as much in common as we have? Our world revolves around dogs, our son, and honey, whether you know it or not, each other. What about it, Robbie? What do you want?"

Robbie stroked his dog's head. "Just to grow up, like a normal kid. I want to watch Dad judge in his ring, and you, Mom, judge in your ring. I want to be a normal family. I don't mind dog shows, and I love our dogs. Can't I just have fun with my dog? Trying to win all the time is too tense.""Laura," Alan's eyes pleaded, but his voice was firm. "Can't we just drop this damned divorce, okay? Life's too short. Let's just make some compromises and love each other."

Laura turned and looked into her estranged husband's eyes. They weren't estranged anymore, and neither was she. As Roxi picked up her head and licked Robbie's face, Laura hugged her husband and said, "Okay."

Willed Accidents Happen

A short story of mystery and suspense, a psychiatrist experiences accidents. But are they?

This story is dedicated to all New Yorkers who've faced violence of any type: Who have fallen down the subway steps in a snowstorm, who've narrowly missed a car bumping them during rush hour, or who've had the rush hour crowd push them so hard, they barely escaped an oncoming subway train.

Ah, the excitement of New York City during rush hour.

This story is also dedicated to my favorite haunts and ex-haunts of the city: The Statue of Liberty, The Cloisters, The Metropolitan Opera, Manhattan School of Music, Bayside, Brooklyn, Lower New York Harbor, and, of course, the grandest and saddest of them all, The World Trade Center. May she rest in peace. And, to the wonderful people of New York.

Life sucked.

Michael Ryan trudged along First Avenue and counted the latest catastrophes.

Cars hurled themselves into his path, and subway trains tried to suck him off the platform. His patient, Jeffrey Ridgeway, had a psychotic break and decided Michael was spawned by the devil. His girlfriend of eight years broke off their engagement.

What the hell else could happen?

Heavy snowflakes fell so thick, they almost obliterated the streetlights. On the sidewalk, someone knocked into Michael, and he slipped on a patch of ice. As he slid, he caught hold of a parking meter, regained his balance, slipped again, and this time hung on. He heaved a sigh of relief. Only the treads on his boots saved him from falling into the rush hour traffic.

As he stepped onto the first concrete step and descended into the Brooklyn-Manhattan Transit Subway Station, he glimpsed at the mass of bodies that pushed behind him. Someone jostled his side, and Michael, treads or no treads, lost his footing, grasped for the iron railing, but somebody else came between Michael and the steel bar. His arms flailed, and he groped the air as he went down feet first.

With no one in front to stop his fall, he bumped down the steps, banged into the center rail, and rolled the last few steps into commuters who streamed out from a train. A woman standing caught his fall and tumbled on top of him as he came to a stop.

Red hair on a body that carried a slight scent of jasmine blocked his vision before the stench of commuter's feet on the concrete, and the moldy walls could overpower his senses. He heard the woman groan as she rolled off his chest. Michael wasn't able to move. He hurt all over.

A crowd of curious onlookers pushed by glared at Michael and the woman on the ground.

"You, okay?" From the corner of his eye, he glimpsed at the young woman who knelt at his side. He might be hurt, but he wasn't dead. She was a redhead and pretty.

A man, sporting tortoiseshell glasses, peered down at him. "Should we call an ambulance?"

The glasses reminded him, where had his own glasses gone?

Michael tried to sit, but the pain forced him back down. He moved his fingers, then his arms. They worked. Nothing broken. His toes scored a number ten for coldness, but he could wiggle them. He thought if he could stay down for a few more minutes, he'd be able to get back onto his feet.

"Move!" An authoritative voice parted the milling crowd until a tall, curly black-haired storm trooper type towered over him.

"Michael Ryan?" The man's expression changed from frown to surprise. A slight upturn in his lips indicated he might smile in a couple of centuries. "Jesus. Michael? What the hell?"

"Ramon? Garcia? Boy, I'm glad to . . . Oh shit."

Michael groaned and rolled onto his side. He tried to get up, but his back muscles spasmed, and he fell back. He reasoned it could have been worse. His heavy-duty parka protected at least some of his body. Nothing broken here. His neck—pinched but intact. Shoulder—ouch. Maybe a nasty bruise.

"My glasses—can't find . . ." He grabbed onto Ramon's shoulder, but he still couldn't get onto his feet.

"No, stay down. I'll call the paramedics." Ramon Garcia waved a badge, shooed away the crowd, and reached in and grabbed his cell phone.

"I'm all right. I just need to get to my feet. And find my glasses."

"We'll find them. And yes, you're going to the emergency room. It's just around the corner."

"Oh hell, no," Michael said, not so sure himself. He risked the consequences. "I know the doctors there. They'll laugh their asses off."

Ramon grabbed his outstretched hands and pulled him to his feet.

Michael's back muscles cramped up again. He cried out as the woman grabbed his other arm.

"Maybe we'd *better* call an ambulance," she said, her voice soft-spoken, throaty—nice. "You might have a concussion."

Despite the his own aches, the woman's voice had a soothing quality. Michael tried to shake his head, but his muscles pinched and tightened.

The two of them changed his mind.

"No concussion, but geez, sore as hell muscles. Okay. I'll go. But I *am* okay. I know who I am."

"Oh, yes? Who are you?" she asked.

"I'm Michael Ryan, psychiatrist. But everyone calls me Michael." There, he still had a sense of humor. "I think I'm thirty-something years old, and I don't have a concussion." He held up four fingers. "See? Four fingers. And, I still have my teeth, I think . . ." He felt them with his tongue. "Yep. And my hair hasn't fallen out." He shook the water from his head. "Matted though it is. God, what a mess."

"Everyone has matted hair with that snowstorm outside. But you do have a nice head of wet hair," the woman said. "I'm partial to dark-headed men with wire-rimmed glasses." She held out his glasses. "Here, these yours? I picked them up."

The initial pain started to subside, and curiosity took over. "And who are you?" he asked.

"Allison Andrews—Allie," she replied. She held on to his arm and smiled. "I'm glad I could be of assistance."

She turned to Ramon. "You have a badge on your belt. Police officer?" Allie looked at him with interest.

"Yes, ma'am. Detective Ramon Garcia." He took her hand and shook it.

"One of New York's finest," Michael added. He tried to get past his injuries with conversation.

"Nice meeting you, Detective Garcia."

He turned back to Michael. "So, we take you to the ER?"

"I wrenched my shoulder," he said, "I'm sore but healable, but yeah. I guess we go."

"Lucky you didn't break your neck," Allie said.

"Yeah, lucky that." He took the glasses and wiped them off with his sleeve. "Thanks. I knew there was a reason I couldn't see anything." He brushed off the subway grime from his coat and wiped the lenses on his sleeve before he put them back on his face.

"I hope I didn't hurt you."

"I'm not as hurt as *you* appear to be," she said. She raised an eyebrow and frowned. "What happened to you, anyway?"

"It must have been the crowd," he replied. "I got pushed from behind. It's a wonder I didn't break any bones falling down those stairs. At least I don't think I . . ."

The roar of a subway drowned out their conversation. As the train came to a stop, a flood of commuters spilled through the turnstile.

Ramon shouted something to Michael, but he didn't hear.

A subway security officer pushed through the crowd. "Hey, I saw what happened. Are you all right?" The man looked out of breath and tucked his shirt back into his pants like he'd been mauled. "Sorry, I didn't get here before this. A crowd blocked my way."

"You saw?" Michael's eyes focused on the man. Then, embarrassed at the spectacle he must have made, he said, "Well, yeah, accidents will . . ."

The man cut him off. "Accident, like hell it was." He looked at Ramon. "Someone pushed him down those stairs."

"Pushed?" Michael flinched back like he'd been struck.

"Pushed," the man repeated. He stared at Michael before he turned back to Ramon.

"Did you see what the guy looked like?" Ramon asked.

The man shook his head. "Some guy, not very tall, kinda sandy hair . . . wore a suit. Can't think of anything that stood out about him. He came down the stairs with the others. I think he wore tortoiseshell glasses."

"Damn," Michael said. "Some guy stood at the foot of the stairs. Same description. I remember those tortoiseshell glasses. He asked me if I was okay."

"Maybe a coincidence."

Somehow, Michael doubted it.

Ramon pulled out a card. "If you think of anything else, give me a call."

The officer read the card, then looked at Ramon and raised his eyebrows. "A detective? So . . ." He pocketed the card. "Should we file a report?"

"And say what?" Michael asked. "That someone pushed me down the stairs, but we don't know who, or even if that happened? I thought I slipped on a patch of ice. I still think so. No one would have a reason to push a perfectly strange person down the subway steps.”

“Unless he was in a hurry, and you were in his way,” the security officer said.

“Or, unless someone has a grudge against you and just happened to be there,” Allie said. She tilted her head. “Does anyone have a beef with you?”

“I don’t think so,” Michael said, not so sure.

“Well, I have your card in case I learn anything. We can still file a report if you want. Here’s my card.” He handed the card to Michael and disappeared through a group of passengers.

“What were you doing in this station?” Ramon asked Michael. “I thought you lived near the Village.”

“Not anymore. I moved to Brooklyn. I take the subway to Bay Ridge.”

“You’re in Brooklyn, now?”

“Yeah,” Michael said. He brushed off his jeans and winced again.

“Michael, you’re in no condition to take the subway. I’ve got my car around the corner. Let me give you a lift. And, we’re going to the ER, then I’ll drive you home. What about you, Allie? Can I drop you off anywhere?”

Allie looked at him with a guarded expression.

“I won’t let anything happen to you on the way, I promise,” Ramon said, with a twinkle in his eyes. “I’ll make Michael ride upfront with me.”

“Oh, I didn’t . . .” she said. Then, she nodded her head and laughed. “Thank you. I’d love a ride. Don’t have a busy social schedule today, so I’ll go to the ER with you.” She grinned. “By a marvelous stroke of luck, I live just across the bridge.”

“Good,” Michael said, at first happy, then . . . Something—just an idea caught his attention. He looked up the subway steps. “Oh hell,” he said. But the thought vanished like the melting ice at the bottom of the stairs.

Three days later, Michael stood in his living room, lost in thought. He stared out the window at the sleet and snow that frosted the scenery and slopped up the sidewalks.

The pain sometimes nagged at him, but not so bad. Just that one back muscle and his bruised shoulder. The Tylenol 3's they'd prescribed for him dulled the physical aches, though not emotional ones.

He'd gone back to work. His patient Jeffrey Ridgeway had been processed into the hospital—finally. A long and challenging day, but the man calmed down. He was safe. So was the world at large.

Now, he agonized over and expelled thoughts that anyone might want to hurt him. The security guard at the subway station could have—must have been mistaken. A jostle triggered by a patch of ice tripped him down those stairs. Nothing more.

He blew his breath onto the window and created a foggy corner.

A simple accident like all the other 'simple' accidents. Michael's own stupid fault he'd had to take the past two days off. He'd worried about his patient, Jeffrey Ridgeway, and the woman he'd loved and lost. Where was she? Did she miss him? Did she already have somebody else? Did she know he'd been hurt? Did she care?

Jeffrey Ridgeway, Susan Richardson. A woman passed his window. Her blonde hair blew in front of her face from the wind. She reminded him of Susan, but the visibility was poor, the window partly iced. He couldn't tell for sure.

At first, he didn't hear his doorbell ring until its incessant clang echoed into his brain. Allie was meeting him here. Maybe it was her? That brightened his moment.

He opened the door, and his eyes widened. It wasn't Allie.

"Susan."

"I didn't think you were home. I rang the doorbell three times." Susan Richardson stood by the open door. She removed her hat, and blonde curls fell down her back. Melting sleet dripped off her blue coat onto the tile in the foyer. She carried a small package.

Michael felt a tug at the hole where his heart used to reside. His lovely Susan. Hair the color of his walls—flaxen wheat. He'd joked he couldn't distinguish her hair from the walls. It was funny at the time. Not so much now.

"Michael." Susan entered the room, and the hole deepened. She slung her purse over the chair, the same as a million times before. The girl put on a carefree performance, yet the hurt reflected from her eyes. She cared for him, all right. But not enough.

She dropped all pretense of a cheerful countenance when she looked at him. "What the hell? What happened to you? What did you do to yourself?" He'd tried to cover a bruise on his cheek, apparently without success.

"I fell down the subway steps. Was off two days."

Her gaze searched his face. "You did what? Why? How?"

"Fell on some ice."

"With those boots you wear? We bought them so you *wouldn't* slip."

He nodded, his mouth tightening. "I know. It was slippery everywhere. Ramon found me at the bottom of the stairs, along with some other people. He carted me over to the ER. My buddies over there got some laughs at my expense." He rolled his eyes. "They thought it was funny."

"Your buddies think everything's funny. They think it's funny whenever anyone they know does something stupid."

His shoulders rose in protest. "Stupid? I got jostled by the rush hour crowd. I slipped on the ice on the stairs. That's all."

Susan nodded. "Okay. I stand corrected. So how are you?" She shook out her hair and removed her coat.

"Been better."

"I . . ."

He watched her lose her nerve. Good. Maybe, she felt something.

"I brought back your engagement ring. You left it at my apartment last week when you left. It was your mother's. I thought you'd . . ." She took a deep breath, ". . . want it back."

"Just put it down over there." He nodded toward the coffee table by the sofa. Despite his effort, his voice came out rougher than intended. He bit his lip, and inside, his stomach turned sour.

"Do we really have to break up over this?" A frown set on her pale face. Her eyes glistened, and a tear worked its way down her cheek.

"It was you who said no," Michael said. He turned away from her. He couldn't go on. He'd dumped her, and it hadn't been fair.

"Michael." Her soft tone bit like the teeth of piranha. "I can't handle marriage right now, that's all. I don't want us to break up. I love you. I just . . ." She gestured with her hands. "Can't manage it. Don't you—?"

The sharp ring of the doorbell cut her off in mid-sentence. They turned toward the opened door as Allie Andrews stood on the threshold. Susan's mouth flew open, stunned. Her expression turned to stone.

"Hi, Michael," Allie said. "Are you ready? Oh."

"Michael," Susan whispered. Her eyes seemed to slap him in the face.

Allie wore a dark green wool coat with a Scottish plaid scarf. Her copper hair spilled down her back, and green, emerald earrings matched eyes that twinkled with life.

By contrast, Susan's were dead.

A small Italian restaurant located on a secluded back street represented only one of New York's famous Greenwich Village's multi-cultural eating establishments.

Old, converted kerosene lamps housed candles to provide romantic light. The waiters wore white shirts with large red and green stripes and matching scarves around their necks like Venetian imports.

They held conversations with their guests, like long-lost friends and family members. Their food warranted such high praise from loyal patrons. Some stopped to eat every evening on the way home from work.

Michael hoped the food critics would stay away, so it would remain an intimate 'hidden treasure.'

"So." He put down the menu on the red and white checkered tablecloth and gave Allie his full attention.

"So, yourself," she said back. "You, okay? Except for the bruise, you look pretty good. Great sweater."

"Really?" Michael smiled. He'd worn jeans with a tan turtleneck sweater for his date with her. His stomach flopped when he realized this had been a present from Susan. *She'd* thought it brought out his eyes. How callous could he be?

"How's your back?"

Michael nodded a lie and shifted positions to get more comfortable. "I have occasional spasms, but I'm healing."

"Do you often fall down subway steps?" The warmth of her smile took away his breath.

When he finally focused, he said, "It's a first for me."

"Well, thank goodness. I thought maybe you picked up girls by knocking them over."

Michael chuckled. "No, I've used some strange pickup techniques in my time, but that was by far the most bizarre."

She looked down and smiled.

He found her extraordinarily attractive and fun—light, not intense. But she entered his life at such a lousy time. He wasn't ready for someone new and hadn't yet resolved his issues with Susan.

He looked up. Allie was talking to him.

"So, what happened, Michael? Did you trip? Get pushed?"

"Don't know. The crowd rushed in from behind. My feet slipped out from under me. You know all that."

Her expression grew so stilled and severe, he couldn't help it. He grinned.

"It's not funny, Michael. You could have gotten killed."

"Maybe I'm accident prone."

"Accident prone? You still think this was an accident?"

"Wait a minute, Allie. You're not buying into the 'someone's trying to get me' routine, are you?"

"Maybe. The security guy seemed to think someone pushed you."

"Probably looked like that to him. No, I wasn't paying attention. I had work on my mind."

"Look, Michael, on the way home yesterday, you mentioned several incidents that happened."

"Yeah, but Allie . . ."

"You nearly got pushed under a subway car," Allie said. She showed no signs of relenting.

"I was thinking about something else."

"Bull," she said. Allie dripped with determination. "You walked across the street and nearly got hit by a car with no headlights."

"Maybe I need to get my glasses changed." Michael took off his glasses, looked through them, moved them away from his face, then closer. "Nope, I can see you perfectly."

She took a deep breath, and her slight frown turned upward into a genuine grin.

"I like to see you smile," he said. He warmed his fingers on the sides of the lantern. A side of his mouth turned up in a half-smile as he looked through the candle flame.

Allie blushed.

The waiter came over to take their order. Michael pushed the candle out of the way. "Allie Andrews, I want you to meet the finest waiter in the City of New York. Tony, meet Allie Andrews."

"Ah, *Benvenuto*. Welcome." Tony beamed, made a grand gesture, and presented his menu.

They couldn't resist the daily special, veal scaloppini, spaghetti, and garlic bread. The man presented his menu like an opera singer who offered a medley of arias. Allie applauded when he'd finished. No other restaurant in New York could compete with Tony and his waiter act. The man left with a bow and a kiss on Allie's hand. Surprise lightened her face. She said, "Tony's a marvelous waiter, Michael. Wherever did you find this place?"

He hesitated. Susan took him here on their first date, and they'd never stopped coming. He wasn't sure why he'd brought Allie.

"Michael?"

"Oh . . . where did I find this place?" He focused back on her face, on those eyes. He thought someone could get lost in the depths of their—What? He jerked back to reality. "A friend of mine took me here. We came here quite a bit."

"Ah, a romance. How long ago?" She spoke in a suffocated whisper as though his answer reflected her future.

"We broke up a couple of weeks ago."

"The girl in your living room."

Michael nodded. "The girl in my living room."

"Oh, the woman. She's pretty, in a sort of tragic way. An Ophelia with long blonde hair and blue jeans. Were you serious?"

"Yes. I wanted to marry Susan. She didn't want to marry me. End of story."

"Oh, Michael, I'm sorry." Somehow, Allie didn't look the least bit sorry.

"Did she—? You don't want to talk about it, do you?"

He shook his head. "No, not really. What about you, Allie? Any boyfriends stashed away?"

"I'm not involved with anyone now if that's what you want to know." Her eyes indicated she might like to be.

He grasped again for a conversation that would lead them in another direction.

"Su . . . Allie," he stopped. He'd nearly called her Susan. "What do you do?"

Allie offered him a tightlipped smile. She'd noticed. Damn.

Allie swallowed. "I'm at NYU. Law. Going for my Ph.D."

"What kind of law?"

"Criminal. My thesis . . . renegade police who kill suspects and what happens to them."

"Interesting," Michael remarked. "My father was a cop. He retired upstate to the mountains. Lucky him."

"Where?"

"Lake George in the Adirondacks."

"Oh, beautiful. My folks live in Scarsdale. They go to the Adirondacks in the summer. Tell me something, Michael, how many of your patients are disturbed enough to be hospitalized?"

Michael stared, completely surprised by her question. Susan cared about that side of his life, and his friends cared about his patients—the small amount discretion would allow, but few strangers would ask. An aspiring lawyer? Maybe. His patients might interest her.

It took a few moments before he replied, "Relatively few, with all the new meds on the market. It's hard to get approval and find empty hospital beds."

"Do you have any out-of-the-ordinary cases?" Allie leaned forward as though conspiring to commit espionage.

Michael leaned back. "I can't give you specifics, but I do have one. Yes, one I recently admitted. He was on meds but forgot to take them. Had a psychotic break. Mad as hell at me at the moment."

"Oh, wow. What kind of symptoms does this man, Jeffrey . . . Michael?"

But Michael only half-heard Allie. A couple walked across the room. The woman had long blonde hair, banded back into a ponytail—Susan's hair, but not Susan.

"You haven't gotten over her, have you?"

"I'm—What? Oh, sorry." Michael focused back on Allie, embarrassed. "I'm a really lousy date."

Allie reached over for Michael's hands. "It's all right, Michael. I know what it feels like to lose someone you love. It's . . . it's like a knife twisted into your heart." Her eyes displayed some sort of inner torment, deep-seated grief. However, when her eyes narrowed, and her face darkened with anger, he wondered why. The words formed on Michael's lips when Allie's attention shifted to the door. Her eyes grew wide, and she grinned. Michael turned around.

Ramon walked up to the table with a nod for Allie and a half-smile for Michael.

"Michael," he said. He nodded to the seat next to Allie. "May I?"

"Hi," Allie said as she made room for him.

"How are you?"

Michael grunted. "Uh, okay, sort of."

"Hi, Miss Allie." He shrugged out of his jacket.

Allie smiled and told him she was just fine.

"What brings you here?" Michael asked. He said it without humor. Ramon Garcia never butted into his dates unless it was necessary. He and Michael worked together whenever the police department needed the advice of a psychiatrist. They were friends, but their paths didn't cross socially much.

"Just doing a bit of undercover here in the Village. Saw you come in." He turned to Allie. "Say, haven't I seen you somewhere before? I can't place you, but I know I've seen your face. Oh yeah, yesterday afternoon. Small world." He grinned, and she laughed.

"My ER buddy, while you were in with your doctor friend," Allie said.

"This isn't your usual area. What gives?" Michael asked.

Ramon's expression stilled and became serious. He tipped his head toward Allie and raised an eyebrow.

Michael caught the hint. "She's okay, Ramon. Anyone who saves my poor excuse for a neck's okay."

"That's why I'm here, Michael. How's your shoulder?"

"Better, but still a bit sore. I'm alive, though. You still think someone has it in for me?"

"You got any enemies?" Ramon pulled his hands through his dark, curly hair. He had the craggy look of an unfinished sculpture.

"Enemies? Only the usual ones any shrink in Manhattan might have, why?"

"Any threats of any kind? Any other accidents besides the incidents you mentioned?"

"No and no. Why? What's this all about?"

"Michael, I went over to your townhouse early this afternoon. Spoke to one of your neighbors. She noticed someone snooping around your house this morning."

Michael shrugged. "So? Delivery people come there all the time. What are you getting at?"

"Your neighbor described the man as the one you saw in the subway. A man with blondish hair-tortoise shell glasses. She said he tried to break in. She screamed at him and let her Doberman out. The dog scared him off."

A muscle quivered in the side of Michael's mouth. Yes, whoever he was, that jerk tried to break in, but wasn't his landlady, Mrs. Bernstein, and her dog fabulous?

Ramon Garcia researched information for his self-appointed mission—to save Michael Ryan. That night, he sat in a cramped little office with a small window overlooking his Manhattan Precinct and wondered what to do next.

He was sure, absolutely sure, those were no accidents. But who and why? He shook his head. Frustrated, he looked for the information he'd requested but found nothing on his desk. He'd gotten back on the phone by the time his overworked administrative assistant hustled in with a stack of computer printouts.

"Thanks," Ramon said. "I owe you."

"Yes, you do," she said. She cocked her head and gave him a crooked smile. "And I intend to collect." The woman pulled her fur hat down over her forehead and wrapped her scarf around her neck. "Don't work too long. Tomorrow's supposed to be your day off. Work too late, you won't be able to get up and enjoy it. Later."

Ramon grunted a "bye" and picked up a file.

The first read, "Ridgeway, Jeffrey." He read all available information on Michael's unstable patient—his arrest for assault on an old woman in the park. He'd thought the devil appointed her to destroy the world. For a while, he'd been okay on prescribed meds. Then, he'd gone off them and attempted suicide by throwing himself into the Hudson River. He'd been hospitalized for that episode but then released due to an overcrowded ward. Next, his allegations that Michael was the child of the devil. He'd lunged for him during one of his sessions. What was with Jeffrey Ridgeway and the devil? He shook his head and read on. Before his illness, Jeffrey had been an actor, a master of disguise. Michael might not have recognized him. He needed to find out where Jeffrey was during that attack. He made a few phone calls.

The second file read "Susan Richardson." He'd known Michael's girl-friend, a New York City School System teacher, and couldn't imagine her involved with attempts on Michael's life. Her parents were still alive, an older retired couple who doted on their only daughter. No problem there.

But they'd recently broken up. Could Susan be vindictive? A matter of, 'If I can't have him, nobody else can?'

Who else had been in her life? Her husband and child had been killed in an accident. Could there be someone else who might connect with her past? A jealous ex-boyfriend, maybe? He re-read the accident file. Her husband had swerved from an oncoming car and ran into a tree. He'd been drinking. Why? Susan's official statement revealed they'd had a fight before the accident. Over what? Ramon read on. An affair with his secretary. Damn. No wonder she didn't want to get married again.

The third file read "Allison Andrews." One brother—Timothy. Some problems here. Petty theft. A small-time arrest record for possession as a teenager.

Andrews. *Where have I heard that name before?* He read through the files—nothing on her. Went to school—graduated with honors. Now, on scholarship at NYU. Mother dead. Killed. Father re-married.

Poor kid, Ramon thought. He was a man dedicated to his own family and felt for anyone deprived of one. Not just dead, though, killed. How? My God, he thought as he read the file. Her mother had been shot. What about other relations? He read on through stacks of names and histories.

Several hours later, Ramon fell asleep on his desk, his head cradled in his arms. He dreamt of Susan Richardson shoving Michael under the subway, Jeffrey Ridgeway pushing him down subway stairs, and Allie Andrews ramming him with her car.

At eight o'clock the following morning, he called Michael's house. No answer. Allie's place? Where was he? He called Allie's number. No answer. Around eight o'clock, Ramon called Michael's father, Thomas Ryan.

"Thomas? *Que Pasa?*" He withstood a barrage of caterwauling on the other end of the phone.

"Sorry, I know it's early. Michael there?"

"He should be on his way. What's up?"

"Will he be alone?"

"Probably. Why?"

"Great. I need to talk to both of you. I'll drive up this afternoon. By the way, Tom, if Michael told you about his *accidents,* don't believe him. They weren't. I think I know who's responsible, but I need some confirmation. Later."

Ramon planned an agenda that included a visit to Michael's clinic, Bellevue Hospital, New York University, and the Catskill Mountains, grabbed his coat, and ran out of his office. He slammed the glass door behind him.

Michael put on a warm fleece-lined coat and scooted out the back door of his townhouse. He tried to outrun heavy raindrops that verified The Weather Channel's prediction of a warmer but lousier and thunderstorm-filled day.

He hopped into the red Corvette he'd bought a month ago. Today, he loved this car more than any woman. Especially the woman with long flaxen hair and powder blue eyes.

Last night—or was it this morning? The phone blasted him out of his sleep. Susan sounded drunk—plastered—bombed. Music and yelling in the background. Where the hell was she? In a bar? Not like Susan at all.

She'd threatened him. The love of his life for seven years, now she wanted to kill him. Maybe he didn't know her as well as he thought he did. She sounded strange. Voice slurred. Then she'd giggle. Then yell. Half-awake, he tried to calm her down, but she hung up. He checked the number—no luck. A payphone from somewhere. This morning, he'd called her house and didn't get an answer. Damn it. Where had she been? She'd broken it off with him. Hadn't she? Well, maybe he'd over-reacted. Maybe he . . .

Thoughts of the red-headed Allie forced Susan from his mind as he started the engine. She was meeting him at his father's house. How had a broken relationship with Susan gone to Allie's meeting his father within a week?

Bizarre. Michael had never fallen for anyone as fast as he had with that red-headed beauty. Was it love? He didn't even know her. He'd just done what he'd counseled dozens of clients not to do. Moving too fast. *Way* too fast.

"Slow down. You move too fast. Have to make the moment last." He hummed. What was the tune? Who'd sung it? Oh yeah. Simon and Garfunkel. "Feeling Groovy."

The smooth purr of the motor blocked out both women for the moment.

He managed to keep accidents and women from his mind as he headed up the Sawmill Parkway, crossed over the Tarrytown Bridge to the New York State Thruway. He restrained the car to a cool 65 mph.

No hint of trouble came until he caught his first glimpse of the Catskill Mountains. The sight always took his breath away. He wasn't paying much attention to the almost non-existent traffic. Out of the corner of his eye, Michael noticed a dark blue Cadillac pull alongside and keep pace with him. Odd. So little traffic. Why so close?

Michael slowed down, so did the Caddy. He sped up, the other car pulled alongside. Michael tried to look over into the vehicle's darkened front window, but the car veered toward him, forced him to keep his eye on the road and change over into the far-right lane.

The highway climbed into the mountains. On the right, a cliff dropped at least fifty feet down into a gorge.

The caddy inched its way over into Michael's Lane.

Michael slammed on the brakes to stay on the road. The Cadillac seemed to spin out of control and almost collided with the Corvette. Michael spun within inches of the cliff before he stopped and waited for the car to push him over the edge.

A semi honked repeatedly as it barreled toward the two vehicles. The Caddy suddenly seemed to regain control and took off. Its tires squealed across the road leaving tracks. The truck slowed and pulled up behind Michael.

The driver slid out and peered in the window with a hard, cold eye. "Are you *nuts?*"

Michael tried to remain calm. An icy fear twisted around his gut, and for a few seconds, he couldn't speak.

The anger lifted from the driver's face. "You, okay?"

"Yeah, I think so. That car. Did you see it?"

"The Cadillac? Yeah, it took off when I stopped. What the hell happened?"

Michael caught the edge in his own voice. "The driver tried to force me off the road. I don't know what was wrong with the creep. He kept inching to the right and pushed me to the edge of the road. Another couple of inches . . ." He took a deep breath and banged on his steering wheel. "Thanks to you, I'm alive right now."

"No problem. Nice 'Vette. My ex-wife has one, got it in the divorce settlement. I drive the old Chevy and my semi. Well, take it easy. Glad you're okay."

Michael sat in the living room of Thomas Ryan's alpine chalet. The large picture window provided an extensive view of the almost invisible Catskill Mountains.

"Even in this weather, she's still beautiful, isn't she? I'm lucky. I've always wanted to retire to the mountains."

Michael smiled. They sat silent for a few moments and sipped Gin and Tonics.

His father continued, "I guess you have other things on your mind than my mountains."

There it was. His father climbed up a notch in talent as a mind reader.

"Dad, what was being a cop like? I mean, did you like it?"

His father raised an eyebrow. "Why? You planning on changing professions?"

"No. I like my job."

Thomas chuckled. "I come from a generation of cops who didn't believe in the practice of psychology for criminal investigations. Times change. I'm proud as hell of you."

Michael shifted positions on a leather lounge chair and swiveled around to look at his dad. His shoulder cramped up, and he flinched.

"What's wrong, Michael? You still in pain?"

"Yeah, steep subway steps." One side of his mouth turned upward. He sighed, shook his head, and said, "Just cramped muscles. It'll heal—eventually."

"Yes, I know," his father said, his voice calm and exact. His eyes didn't waver from his son's face. "How did you manage to fall?"

"I don't know. I guess I tripped."

"How come? You're not accident prone, are you?"

"God, Dad, no. I'm just thinking about other things, that's all. Pre-occupied."

His father chuckled. "Like your patients?"

Michael nodded. "Yeah, like my patients. Can't help thinking I could have helped him from going into a psychotic breakdown. Why can't I recognize the symptoms? Why couldn't I see this coming?"

"Why, why, why? Sometimes there's no signs. They mask it well. So do criminals. Don't beat yourself up over this, Michael. And just because you're in another world right now . . . well, you know the old cliché."

Michael grinned. "Yeah, just because you're paranoid doesn't mean someone's not out to get you. I've never seen myself as the paranoid type."

"Hell, you're not. Never were. Preoccupied, though. Yes. Your head was always in a book. I guess I should talk. Look what happened to me."

Michael's smile faded. He looked down at the floor. "Yeah. Mom. God, that was an awful time." Tears formed. Cancer took her. They knew she was terminal—fading. Still, when death came, they weren't prepared.

Thomas's eyes grew sad, and his lips turned down. "Yes. Fuckin' miserable, period. I ended up in the same hospital where she'd just died. Talk about irony. Thank God you were there for me. I'm not sure I could have made it alone."

The day after his wife died, an armed robbery on the East Side of New York left Thomas Ryan with a bullet injury that fractured a bone in his leg. It led to his eventual retirement. He could walk well enough most of the time, but arthritis forced him to hobble when it rained. His father did quite well, considering all the old injuries from his cop days, including arthritis in his hands. Hell growing old, Michael thought, but he's as sharp as he ever was.

"You know I'll always be there for you," Michael said. "Still, I feel like a disaster area," Michael said. "I just don't get this."

"You mentioned all these accidents have happened in the past two weeks?"

"It started two weeks ago when a crowd pushed too close behind me on the platform. I nearly fell on the tracks in front of a train."

"Damn," his father said.

"The next day . . ." Michael relived the event that left him shaking for hours. "I crossed First Avenue after work around ten o'clock. I could hardly see the streetlights because of the fog. A car came out of nowhere. No headlights, nothing."

"That doesn't sound like an accident," his father said, his tone now edged with steel. "It sounds deliberate."

"Who'd do that on purpose?" Michael asked.

An unpleasant twist crossed his father's mouth. He lowered his voice to almost a whisper. "You'd be surprised."

Michael started and almost wrenched his neck, looking at his father.

"Then you fell down the subway steps?"

"Yeah. I met Allie. Nothing's happened since I met her."

"Love at first fall?" Thomas asked. A smile fell across his ruddy face, and he sat back and stared.

"She's nice," Michael said. He looked down and dusted some lint off his jeans. He knew what was coming.

"What about Susan?"

"It's over." The pain hit the pit of his stomach as he thought about Susan. Something about those icy-blue eyes. Beautiful—tragic.

"She wasn't ready for a commitment," he continued. "I tried. I really wanted to marry her. I loved her. You liked her—Mom liked her. But, yes, it's over. "

"Too bad. Susan's a nice girl," Thomas said. "You sure you didn't rush her a bit? She hit bottom after the death of her family. You don't get over a loss like that overnight."

"Yeah, I know. Susan let me know she needed so much space. There wasn't room for me. So, I gave it to her." He shifted in his seat, put his hands together in a steeple-like position, and pressed them on his bottom lip. "And we've been together for a long time. You'd think she could move on. If she really loved me, wouldn't she know me well enough to know if I was the right man for her?"

"Maybe, but you've been in school, then started your career." His father sat silent for a moment, then tilted his head. "Michael, you know I try not to interfere with your life, but Susan reminded me of your mother in a lot of ways. And I think she liked you—a lot." He coughed. "And, you know, you're not getting any younger. I know all the schooling you had. You and Susan were together for a lot of years. I was hoping for grandkids before I died." He smiled. "You're thirty-two now." He stared out over the mountains.

Michael scrambled to respond to the 'you were getting over the hill speech' when his dad changed the subject. "You mentioned nearly being in an accident on the toll road this morning. What happened?"

"A driver must have hit a wet patch on the road because he swerved into my lane and nearly sent me over a cliff. If I'd gone off, I would have plunged fifty feet."

Michael swiveled back toward the window. The mountains became visible once again, white tops against a copper and steel sky. He heard the rumble of thunder in the distance. Crazy weather for the middle of April. One-minute snowstorms, the next thunderstorms.

"I hate to be the bearer of bad tidings. As I see it, these haven't been accidents." His father's voice held a serious undertone.

"They must be accidents," Michael said. He swiveled back. "Anything else would be too bizarre to even think about."

"Well, son. Start thinking." Thomas's eyes met Michael's before Michael looked away.

"Take that patient you've mentioned. Could he be mad at you? What about other patients?"

"Dad, this is stupid. Even Ramon thinks someone's out to get me. It's nuts—paranoiac."

"Damn it, Michael. You don't run out in front of traffic, and you don't trip over your own feet in the subway station. As far as . . ."

The doorbell rang. Michael pushed himself up from the chair, freed from the lecture that would follow.

"That'll be Allie," he said. He started for the door. "I'm dying for you to meet her."

"Why didn't she drive up with you?" Thomas half stood, braced against the arm of the chair.

"She has relatives in Scarsdale."

Allie stood in the doorway with a bright smile and a bottle of wine. When Michael greeted her, she kissed him then pulled away as she saw his father.

Thomas coughed.

"Dad," Michael said, "This is Allie. Allie, meet my father, Thomas Ryan."

Thomas extended his hand, but Allie's held a bottle of wine. "Here," she said. She handed Thomas the bottle. "Michael said you made the best spaghetti on the East Coast. So, I thought I'd bring some Chianti to go with it."

"Thank you, Allie. That's very nice, and it's nice to meet you." Thomas smiled and started to bark orders.

"Michael, get this young woman a drink. What would you like?"

"Oh, thanks. Maybe a Gin and Tonic, if you have it? It's been a long drive."

"Have it? We're drinking it." Thomas escorted Allie into the living room. "How do you like my mountain?" He ushered her over to the picture window. "It's the reason I bought the house."

The outside world looked forlorn and cold. A shiver ran down Michaels' spine—a premonition that something ugly was about to happen. He tried to shake it off. This was supposed to be a fun evening, not a downer. A trickle of raindrops splintered off the window.

Allie smiled and nodded. She stared out the window and then turned back.

"I understand you were on the police force, Mr. Ryan," she said. And then they were off engrossed in conversation.

Michael looked at Allie and his father. Thomas answered Allie's questions, but all the time probed with his stare, probably an instinctive reaction from his years on the force.

Allie seemed to know the right things to say. She made an impression. He watched her wrest control of the conversation, asking questions about Thomas's career on the force. She'd nod at the answers, pick up a thread and ask another.

Michael tried to keep his eyes off her but found he couldn't. He contrasted Allie with Susan. Susan inspired a down-home prettiness. The proverbial 'girl next door.'

But this lady radiated 'gorgeous.' She was tall with high cheekbones and creamy peach skin. Her red hair hung shoulder-length, with one side curled around her ear.

Something else about her caught his attention. The same thing he'd picked up in the restaurant the other night. What was it about her? *Who* did she remind him of?

She wasn't at all like Susan. And why did Susan even enter his mind? Why couldn't he get *her* out of his thoughts? And that damned phone call. He wasn't about to tell *anybody* about that, including his father.

"I understand you two met at a subway station," Thomas said.

"Yes," Allie said, with mischief in her voice, "Michael literally fell for me."

Thomas couldn't contain himself, and he roared with laughter. "Here's to you, young lady," he said. He raised his glass to her. "You're quick. Good for you. What do you do for a living?"

"I'm getting a doctorate in Criminal Psych from NYU. Last fall, they offered me a scholarship. I'm two months into the program."

"So, you're from New York? I detect the delicate strains of the famous New York accent, but also a bit of Boston thrown in."

Allie grinned and said, "Yes, sir. I'm from New York, born and bred. I did some undergrad work at Boston U. My folks live in Scarsdale. They wanted me to move in with them, but my brother and I moved to Brooklyn instead."

"Wow, I'm impressed. Great background. You know Michael's a psychiatrist. You two should be good for each other. He can help you in your studies." He toasted his glass to them. They drank in silence for a minute.

"What do you think about Michael's accidents?" Allie asked.

"We've been discussing them," Michael said. "I'm the only one who seems to think they *were* accidents."

"Well, I don't believe any of them were accidents," she replied.

"I don't either. Too much coincidence—and that car that tried to push him off the road this morning—"

"This morning?" Allie put her drink on the cocktail table and faced Michael.

"Oh, come *on,* Allie, it wasn't anything," he insisted.

"No?" asked his father. "Michael nearly got run off into a ravine on his way up here."

"Yes, I'd think that was something."

Michael sighed, tired of all the explanations. "Just some idiot who figured he'd like to race a Corvette and lost control."

"Bull!" Allie's eyes flashed a 'don't be so stupid' look.

After a spaghetti dinner, garlic bread, and Chianti, they sat at the table and played Yahtzee. They laughed until they cried and interspersed their conversation with stories about their childhood.

"It's a shame you lost your mother at such an early age." Michael's tone turned serious.

Allie folded her hands and looked at them. "We lived in Brooklyn, just across the bridge. Near where Tim and I live now."

She looked away and avoided eye contact, her eyes clouded.

"Mom worked as a journalist for *The Village Voice*. She always looked young. I guess she didn't look like a reporter. She had long red hair and hoop earrings. That's what I remember most about her, those earrings.

"She fit in with the artistic crowd in the East Village. Someone reported drug trafficking, and the police raided one of the apartment buildings. My mother covered the story, her last assignment." A tear sprung from Allie's eye. "Somebody killed her. The police, I believe."

"My God." Thomas seemed to relive something, and he banged his fist on the table. The dice jumped. "I was there," he said. "They ambushed the police from the upper floors. It took a while before they got the guys, a pathetic mixture of hippies, junkies, and a drug dealer named Ben Logan. Biggest bust in years. I led the task force that brought them down. They shot at my men but finally surrendered after several of them were wounded. I don't remember anyone killed, though." Thomas shook his head and frowned.

"She must have gotten into the line of fire," Allie said, her eyes cast down on the table. "She ended up in the hospital, then died a few days later. At any rate, I no longer had a mother." Everyone sat silent for a minute. The game of Yahtzee came to a halt. Michael took her hand and held it tight. Allie sighed, regained her hand, and continued. "Dad re-married a year later. She tried hard to be a good mother. Sometimes I almost let her. Perhaps I wasn't quite fair."

"Don't be so hard on yourself," he said. "Losing your mother like that's an awful thing for a child." He lowered his voice. "Actually, it's hard for someone of any age."

Michael remembered the loss of his own mother. It had been hard on him, but his father had taken it even harder.

They sat silent. Michael fought for the right words to say and came up empty.

The phone rang—a welcome distraction. Michael plucked it from the buffet behind the table.

"Hello?"

The voice on the other end wanted to speak to Allie. Surprised, he handed her the phone. "It's for you."

She raised her eyebrows. "Hello? Oh, hi there. I'm here at a wonderful chalet near Lake George with a quaint wooden balcony surrounding the second story. It's darling." She smiled at Thomas, and Thomas grinned back. Allie made an impression.

"We just finished dinner. Having a great time. Thanks for calling." She handed the phone back to Michael.

"That man needs to get a life. Would you believe my brother wanted to make sure I'd arrived, okay?" She shrugged.

Michael thought her brother would hear more about this later. "Well, it's nice he cares enough to make sure you're okay."

Allie picked up the dice. "So, let's play some more. I'm getting the hang of it."

The phone rang again. Michael grabbed it again.

"Sylvia! What's up?" He flinched at the sound of his secretary's voice. She seldom ever called with good news.

"Dr. Ryan, sorry to disturb you, but I thought you ought to know Jeffrey walked out of the hospital and disappeared."

A cold chill ran down Michael's spine. He raised his voice an octave. "How the hell did *that* happen?"

"An orderly walked him out the door."

"Just like that?" Michael fumed. "When did this happen?"

"This morning around nine o'clock."

He frowned and drew his eyebrows together. "Why the hell didn't you call me?"

"Dr. Ryan." Sylvia's tone turned accusatory. She formed her words like she might speak to a ten-year-old. "You turned your cell phone off. I've left four messages at your house and two on your mobile," she explained. "You obviously didn't pick them up. I finally looked up your father's number."

"My cell phone." Oh yeah. Damn. He'd turned it off.

"Where was he headed?"

"We called in the police in case he might come after you," she said. "But nobody's seen him."

"Okay. Thanks for letting me know. You need me to come back?"

"No. You're better off away from here."

"Okay. Let me know if anything happens."

When Sylvia said she would, Michael pressed the button down on the phone and put it on the table next to his seat. He pulled out his cell phone from his jacket pocket, clicked the 'on' button, and put it back.

He sat and looked at his father and Allie. Both stared at him with curiosity.

"Jeffrey Ridgeway escaped from the hospital and disappeared."

Thomas's face showed a 'Yeah, so what?' look.

"Somebody walked him out while they were waiting to admit him. He's threatened to kill me on more than one occasion." He ran his fingers through his hair, exhaled, and shook his head. His nerves got the better of him. "The police are looking for him. They'll catch him."

Allie raised her eyebrows. "Okay," she said, "You have your mysterious Mr. X, the one who tried—has been trying to do you in all week." She rolled her dice. "Five sixes. Yahtzee."

Michael threw the dice. "Hm, a full house, just what I needed. He couldn't have done them all. I called into the hospital at nine o clock. He'd just arrived."

"Maybe this morning was an isolated incident by a stupid—or drunk driver," his father said. "Yahtzee again. It's all in your wrist, Allie. Maybe Ridgeway did the rest."

"No, he couldn't have. My department was evaluating him at the time I fell down into the subway."

Allie's turn again. "Oh darn," she said as she rolled three fives and two threes. "I have no place to put this."

"How about chance?" Thomas suggested.

"All out." She scratched out a box on her score sheet. "Maybe he has an accomplice," she said.

"Who? His family believes he needs hospitalization. Besides, Jeffrey doesn't wear tortoiseshell glasses."

"But he's an actor," Thomas said. "He'd have disguises."

The phone rang again. Michael grabbed it.

"Hello."

The blood rushed to Michael's head, and his heart almost stopped. He looked at Allie. "Hi, Susan," he said.

He listened to her melancholy melodic voice that reminded him of their visit to his father—together. She wanted to come even though they'd broken up.

He'd have rather chewed on glass than said, "No, I can't tonight."

"Oh," she said. "You mean you brought the new girlfriend? She's met your father already?" Her bitterness bit through the distance of their phone call.

"Hold on. That's not fair. You broke this off, not me. I gave you an *engagement* ring, remember?"

"Yes, you did," she conceded. "But I didn't break up with you, Michael. I loved . . . love you."

"Look . . ." Michael got up from his chair and excused himself. He walked across the dining room into the far corner of the living room. "My father isn't feeling well. He isn't up for any company."

"Oh, so she's not there," Susan replied.

Michael didn't respond. "Where are you now?" he asked. The rain pelted the roof, heavier now. He could barely see the outline of the lake.

"Visiting my parents."

He didn't think so. He heard a loon in the background, and Susan's parents didn't live by a lake.

"Look, I'll be here overnight. We'll talk tomorrow," Michael said. He put his hand close to the speaker. "And why did you call me at three this morning? Where were you? You sounded drunk." He'd toned his voice down to almost a whisper.

He turned to look at Allie while he spoke to Susan. She and his father hadn't taken their eyes off him. He turned his back.

Susan said, "What do you mean, I called you at three in the morning? Are you hallucinating? Anyway, about tomorrow, we'll see." A calm resignation replaced the former hostility. She hung up. Michael faced the dial tone. He mouthed, "Damn."

"I'm not feeling well," Thomas said. "What's wrong with me? I thought I felt fine." He rolled the dice, and Michael went back to the table and sat. Allie and Thomas stared at him.

"You heard."

"Yep, pretty much everything, except for that last part," his father said. "This house wasn't built for secrets."

"No, I guess not." Michael reached his arm over the table and took Allie's hand. "Look, I'm sorry. It wasn't the right time to explain that I have a new girlfriend. She doesn't need that now."

"Maybe she does," Allie said, her tone drawn in sympathy. She removed her hand. "There's nothing like a little competition to get the adrenaline going."

"Let's play Yahtzee." Michael shook his head and then shook the dice. They played another game and Michael won this time.

The lights flickered. As they dimmed, the rain hit the window, steadier and harder. Michael thought he saw a shadow move past the window. "Just a minute," he said. "I'll be right back." Michael stood up to look.

"What's wrong?" Thomas got up and followed him.

A gunshot roared through the dining room window and missed both by inches.

"Everybody, down!" Thomas exploded

Nobody needed to hear him a second time. They dove under the table as the residue of rain blew in, followed by a bright flash of lightning hit simultaneously with a loud crash of thunder. The lights went out.

"Damn, Michael, the guns are in the study."

"I'll try to get to them."

Furniture became an obstacle course as Michael bumped his way into the study toward the gun cabinet. He felt around the door frame for the switch. When he clicked it on, nothing happened.

He thought he heard a noise and spun around and held his breath. Nothing.

The drawers of his father's antique bureau lay just beneath the cabinet. When he finally found it, Michael hit his elbow on the corner of the chest. *Damn!* A pain shot up his arms, and he bit his tongue to keep quiet.

He fumbled around to find the drawer handle and managed to pull open the top drawer to reach inside. A flashlight—with batteries. He flipped on the switch. Not strong, but bright enough. He shone the light on bullets and clips stored in the drawer. Then he reached up to the gun cabinet and picked out two suitable weapons.

The noise from the other side of the room startled him again. He pointed one of the guns and inched his way to the other side of the room. Rain blew in through another open window. Michael crawled over and peered out. Frothy waves above an inky black lake darkened the windows, and the shadows of trees flickered on the edge of the porch. A hint of lightning flashes shown visible mountain peaks. Other than the swaying tree branches, he saw no movement, just heard the breathing of the wind. He tried to close the window, but it wouldn't budge. Stuck—damn it!

The rain blew in and drenched his face.

He backed up and almost made his way back through the room without killing himself when he collided into the corner of a desk with his knee. He saw stars as the thunder crashed closer.

Michael limped back into the dining room, hunched over, out of window range. "Dad, Allie," he whispered.

"Over here." His father covered Allie with his body under the dining room table.

Michael handed his dad a gun. "Whatever you do, Allie, stay down," he said. "Whatever this is about, it doesn't have anything to do with you."

"Unless they don't want any witnesses," she replied.

Michael listened for movements. The noise of the thunder and rain made it hard for him to hear—anything. Strangely, one side seemed to have a heavier movement than the other. They sounded like footsteps that stomped across the house. Then, he realized a chalet roof sloped too much for anyone to walk on it—especially in the rain. The sounds came from upstairs.

"Get into the study and *stay there*," Michael said. "The window's open in case you have to get away."

"Michael, no! You're not equipped to handle this type of situation." Thomas gripped his son's arm.

"Let me go. Dad, this isn't your fight."

"We don't know whose fight it is."

"Yes, we do. It's mine. Besides . . ." They both knew. Thomas could no longer manage physical conflicts. "Take Allie into the study. Let me handle this."

Thomas let go but didn't move. He couldn't see his father's face, but he heard his uneven shallow breathing—smelled his fear. Then, he and Allie disappeared.

Michael inched his way to the stairs close to the edge of the wall. He heard the movement again, this time centered, at the head of the stairs. A dark figure against a gray-black background appeared in the flash of lightning then disappeared back into the inky void. At least he knew where the enemy was when the bullet whizzed inches from his face. He brought his arms close into his chest and shot back.

What was his father thinking? "Get down!" Michael yelled. Out of the corner of his eyes, he saw two figures at the entrance of the study.

He turned back to an empty hallway when the form came back into view. Another shot rang out and catapulted into an oak beam that ran from the ceiling to the floor. It shot a hole through Thomas's dartboard.

Michael shot back.

"Jeffrey?" Michael tried on his psychiatrist's hat. Maybe reason with him? He thought he'd risk it.

"Jeffrey. Put the gun down. We'll talk this out. Shooting me will only make matters worse."

No answer.

Michael positioned himself near the edge of the stairs. Another shot zinged past, and he flew back against the wall.

"Whew . . . close." He turned to fire again. There wasn't anyone there. Where had Jeffrey gone? Back into another bedroom? Michael started up the stairs, aware that the creature could spring from inside any room any second. But when the next shot rang out, it came from downstairs.

"Drop it, Michael!"

The voice came from behind him. As Michael spun around, the electricity came back on, and the bright lights almost blinded him. He got a clear view of the man at the top of the stairs, his gun pointed down at Michael. Michael turned back toward the shots. Allie had a gun pointed at his father, and Michael dropped the weapon.

"Allie, *no!*" It didn't register for a second that the beautiful Allie Andrews had the hate of the devil plastered on her face, serious as a demon about firing a bullet into his father's head.

Allie replied, "Let's all go sit down in the living room, shall we?"

"Allie, no . . ." Michael faltered.

"You heard the lady. Let's go sit down." The man in black started down the stairs.

Confused, grieved, and angry, Michael followed his father into the living room. Thomas sat on the massive leather sofa and Michael on the lounge chair. Allie and the figure dressed in black jeans, a turtleneck, and a black leather jacket stood next. The man had sandy blonde hair and wore tortoiseshell glasses.

"Good work, Allie," The man said.

"Let me introduce you," Allie said. "My brother, Timothy Andrews."

"Allie, what's this all about?" Michael asked, tormented by fear and mixed emotions. What *was* this all about?

"It took me years to find out who murdered my mother. I found him," Allie said.

"Who? What do you mean?" Michael stared at Allie, puzzled. He couldn't read anything from her face—Her expression resembled a mask.

"It was hushed up, wasn't it, Mr. Ryan? But you did it. I read the records. I made it a point to find out who participated in that raid and who was *so quick* to pull the trigger on an innocent reporter. You fired the shot that killed my mother."

Thomas, who'd been pale anyway, blanched like a corpse.

"You never even bothered to check to see what happened to her. My mother was a journalist, for God's sake. A young woman with two children. Tim and I wanted you to know what it feels like to lose a son before I shoot *you*."

Allie's mask lifted and showed her grief-stricken obsession. "Like . . . like you did to my mother."

Timothy looked over at his sister. He showed nothing but the self-righteous rage of the insane. "Allie, cool it."

Thomas said, "Allie, let's talk about this. Put the guns down, both of you."

"I'm afraid not." Timothy's voice growled—a hard and cold sound. It blended well with the icy rain that now poured horizontally against the windows.

Allie reacted to Timothy's voice, the swift shadow of her own fury that swept across her face. Michael stared into the eyes he'd thought so full of life. Those eyes—what they reminded him of—Jeffrey Ridgeway when he got lost in his own reality.

Susan Richardson entered through the study window, positive nobody heard her car over the racket of the weather. Unfortunately, once open, the window stuck, and she couldn't shut it again.

When someone entered the room, she crept behind the desk, prayed the lights wouldn't come on, and whoever the intruder was wouldn't try to shut the window. When he did, she recognized Michael and held her breath.

She thought he'd heard her breathing but then had chalked it up to the wind. When he left, she edged her way across the room with her knee to prevent knocking into the furniture like Michael had.

She huddled behind the door and waited, listening to the gunfire. Peering through the crack in the door jam, she saw the red-headed Allie and some man brandish guns. This would never do. Nobody would shoot Michael before she had a chance at him.

"Thomas, we'll make this as painless as possible for your son. Something you, sir, didn't offer our mother." Allie backed away. She cocked her pistol at Michael's head, ready to fire.

Michael's life flashed before his eyes. He thought about the lousy way he'd treated Susan. All too late. He closed his eyes and waited for his ascent into heaven or his descent into hell when he heard the rush, an intake of breath, and a cry. When he opened his eyes, a blur rushed across the room, out of what appeared to be nowhere.

Allie fired, but the shot went wild as the whirlwind tackled, threw Allie to the floor, and knocked the wind out of her. As Timothy spun around, Michael lunged and knocked him to the ground. The gun flew off to the side. Timothy's hands went up over his head as he lay staring up at him.

The stranger in a ski cap struggled with Allie and had the advantage of surprise. The attacker grappled for the gun and wrenched it from Allie's hand. Allie rolled over—grabbed it back. It went off, firing wildly into the air. Allie turned the gun toward her opponent's head.

Hands and arms tangled, wrestled for control before somebody pulled the trigger.

Everyone sat motionlessly. Allie and her brother lay still, blood everywhere. Michael and Timothy didn't move.

The stranger sat up and pulled off the ski cap, and a long blond braid fell out over her jacket. She managed to smirk.

"Susan!" Michael and Thomas spoke in one voice.

"Hi, guys. How are my favorite heroes? Sorry, if I'd known you had company, I wouldn't have come."

Susan stood and looked down at the gorgeous and very dead Allie Andrews. She gasped and whispered, "Oh my God. I killed her. Oh my God." She turned a tornado shade of sky-green and wretched.

Thomas grinned at her and picked up the phone.

Ramon Garcia popped in around eight o'clock after Timothy Andrews and his sister's body had been hauled off.

"Sorry I missed all the action," Ramon said. He sat at the table drinking scotch. "I should have told you about the Andrews' over the phone. I thought it would have been better in person. You and Susan were supposed to . . . I didn't think Allie would come up here today."

"Don't worry about it," Michael said. "I wouldn't have believed you anyhow."

"Damn it," Thomas asked. They turned toward him. "I can understand them coming after me, but why take it out on you?"

"Revenge. Those two wanted to hurt you, the way you'd hurt their mother," Ramon replied.

"Something she left out, though," Thomas said. "Her mother might have been a reporter, but she wasn't on duty that night. She was *part* of the *drug* crowd. They were all stoned and crazy when they came out of the building." Thomas hesitated and shook his head before he continued.

"The ironic thing about it," Thomas said, "I didn't kill her. I tried to prevent a colleague from pulling the trigger but caught his hand too late. He shot her."

"What about Allie?" Susan looked at Ramon and then glanced at Michael.

Ramon said, "It wouldn't have taken much for Allie and her brother to trace Thomas Ryan and find out he had a son. When they found out Michael was single, they created a suitable situation, and Allie moved in."

"How the hell did he get upstairs?" Thomas asked.

"Dad," Michael said. "You don't exactly lock your windows. Allie gave away the balcony to her brother when he phoned her. It would have been easy for him to get up there."

"With his sister's death," Ramon added, "Andrews broke down and spilled his guts. He pushed you down the stairs at the subway, and Allie caught you. They'd watched you—followed you. Trouble is," he said through a sly grin, "you wouldn't cooperate. That wasn't sporting of you."

"Funny."

"Sorry. I know you liked Allie. It should have been different," Ramon said.

Michael frowned and glanced at Susan's saddened expression.

Ramon flushed and looked down at the floor.

The phone brought them out of an awkward situation.

"Not again," Thomas answered it. "For you." He handed the phone to his son.

Michael raised his eyebrows in question. "Hello? Oh, Sylvia, now what?"

"Dr. Ryan, Jeffrey's back, under heavy guard." She explained what happened.

"Thank God," Michael said. "I'll call you when I get back to town."

When he'd put down the phone, he said, "That was Sylvia. Jeff Ridgeway was found driving out of control on the tollway. He's okay but raving and hallucinating. He says he'd been kidnapped by FBI agents. They've taken him back to Bellevue. He drove a car he says he doesn't own. He can't explain how he got in it."

Thomas handed him a cup of coffee. Ramon nodded. "Thanks. Most welcome." He stirred in some cream. "Well, Timothy kidnapped him, of course," Ramon said. "He went into the hospital this morning dressed as an orderly. Jeffrey made a convenient scapegoat. I'm sure if their plan had succeeded, Jeffrey would have been found dead somewhere."

"So, if Timothy was at the hospital, who tried to run you off the road?" Thomas asked.

"Allie," Ramon said.

"She doesn't drive a Cadillac. I didn't notice—"

"No, but there's one parked in your driveway. Probably stolen. They expected to kill you two and get away in a car that couldn't be traced back to them. Timothy's car isn't in the parking lot. I'll bet you'll find he parked it in town, and she picked him up. He'd been waiting in that car since Allie arrived."

"Allie," Susan whispered. "So, you found a new girlfriend in record time."

Ramon and Thomas scrambled out of the dining room.

"Not exactly. Allison found me." His excuse sounded lame even to him.

"You dumped me, Michael." Susan looked down at the table and avoided his eyes. "And then you went and found someone the next day. Or maybe you'd been going out with her all the time."

"No!" Michael nearly shouted. "I just met her. I wanted to *marry you*. You said *no*." Michael sighed and shook his head. "I'm sorry, Susan. I didn't handle this well."

"Damn it, Michael." Susan got up from the table and turned her back on him. Then she turned back. "I said no because I needed *time* to get used to the idea." Her look stated, 'you bastard.'

Michael cringed.

"When I lost Jack and Evie, I thought my life was over. Especially the pain of knowing my husband was having an affair. I was afraid . . ."

"History would repeat itself?" Michael asked softly.

Susan sighed and nodded. Maybe, as Allie had stated, Susan was a tragic Ophelia. But this one, Michael noted, had fangs. This Ophelia would never have drowned herself. She'd have rescued Hamlet from himself.

"I would never be unfaithful to you. You should know that."

Susan slumped down, and her voice broke, "Should I? You managed to find Allie fast enough."

"I'll admit she was attractive." He looked into her tear-stained eyes that questioned. "I swear, Susan, I didn't sleep with her." There, he'd said it.

The corners of Susan's mouth turned up a little with the beginning of a smile, and she sat back at the table.

"I never stopped thinking about you," he said. He reached over for Susan's hands. She pulled away.

"Why did you decide to come up here today?" Michael asked, numb with anticipation. "And why did you call me last night. Did you call from a bar?" He liked having a little bit of blame shifted to her. "And were you drunk?"

"Drunk?" Susan was indignant. "I was not *drunk*. And I didn't call you. Must have been the red-haired witch who may be lying in the morgue right about now."

Michael sighed. "Well, somebody called me last night. I was half-asleep. Maybe it was her. She shifted the suspicion onto you." He looked deep into the expression of her face and those powder blue eyes. Love lay in there. Anger, yes. But love. And he loved her.

Michael remembered another Allie statement. 'There's nothing like a little competition to get the adrenalin to flow.' Maybe Allie had had a purpose, after all.

"Do you still want to marry me?" Susan whispered.

He took her hand and caressed her knuckles with his thumb. She didn't pull away. "Of course, I do."

But then he shot her a look as he sat back. "You could have been killed."

"Michael," Susan said, "I wasn't about to let that bitch shoot you before I had the chance."

POEM: Razz Upon the Sheep

Photo by Patricia A. Guthrie of Bruce Berg and Razz at a dog walk-a-thon. With apologies and profound admiration to Mr. Ernest Thayer and his wonderful poem "Casey at the Bat." Also, in tribute to the wonderful collie Razz and, among his marvelous accomplishments, his ability to herd sheep. A tribute to a wonderful dog, handler, and two herding instructors.

The outlook wasn't brilliant for the Mudville nine that day;
The score stood four to two with six more sheep to play.
And then when Kippy slid in mud and Glory did the same,
A sickly silence fell upon the handlers in the game.

A straggling few got up to go in deep despair, the rest
Clung to that hope which springs eternal in the human breast;
They thought if only Razz could but somehow become loose,
We'd put up even money now on Razzy and on Bruce.

But Annie preceded Razzy, as did also little Zuri
And the former is too overweight, and the latter is a fury
So upon that stricken multitude, melancholy hit too deep
For there seemed but little chance for Razz to go and
Herd the sheep.

But Annie drove a single sheep, right to her rightful owner
And Zuri, the much-spoiled girl, split the rams into the corner.
And when the ooze had settled, and they saw what had occurred
There was Alex going 'away' and driving back the herd.

Then from handlers and their dogs, there rose a lusty yell,
It rumbled through the farmyard and to the street as well.
It knocked upon the barn door and recoiled upon the deep;
For Razzie, mighty Razzie was advancing to the sheep.

There was ease in the collie's manner as he stepped into that field
There was pride unto his bearing, as Bruce called him out to heel.
And when responding to the cheers, he politely lifted his leg,
No stranger in the crowd could doubt, 'twas Razz, who would not beg.

All eager eyes were on him as he crawled into the dirt,
All tongues were immediately silent as mud smeared upon his skirt.
Then while the writhing sheep regrouped, and one fell on his hip
Defiance gleamed in Razzie's eye. A sneer curled Razzie's lip.

In vans crammed frozen people, all screaming, muffled roars,
As the dog crept by command to the pen's far distant shores.
The rams all sensed the danger and in one mad, frightened pack,
They turned upon poor Razzie for one huge and terse attack.

With a care of circumspection, the sheep he went a round.
As one came on old Razzie bumped that sucker to the ground.
Bruce signaled him to 'come' around, and once more 'round they flew,
But Razzie, he ignored them as the sheep said "baa-aa" to you.

With a heart filled full of instincts and a handler mighty near,
The dog was animated, and to all that came quite clear.
He turned and drove the strays away and straight back to the pack,
The herd itself knew not what hit, as he drove them there and back.

And when the mud and sludge were slimed upon both dog and man,
And sheep in angry group were held by the trainer we called 'Nan.'
Scott, owner of the sheep and flock, a grin upon his face,
Said, "Bruce and Razz will hereafter be the guardians of this place."

About Patricia A. Guthrie

"Every experience is potential fodder for a novel.," says Patricia A. Guthrie. Guthrie is an accomplished musician: opera singer, church soloist, and music teacher. After leaving the opera, she became a music therapist in a school for special needs children and taught music in the Chicago Public School system.

She is the author of romantic suspense novels, mysteries, and short stories. Her novels include *Legacy of Danger, In the Arms of the Enemy, and Waterlilies Over My Grave.* Her short stories appear in online literary magazines *L'Affaire du Coaeur* and *Skyline Magazine.* Her non-fiction articles appear in *Collie Cassette* and *Nature Journal.* A member of Fresh Ink Group, you can find her at FreshInkGroup.com and on her own website, PaGuthrie.wordpress.com.

Patricia kindly asks that, if you enjoyed these stories, please leave a review on Amazon, GoodReads, Barnes and Noble, or any of the other retailers. Reviews are what keep authors alive.

Fresh Ink Group
Independent Multi-media Publisher
Fresh Ink Group / Voice of Indie / GeezWriter / Push Pull Press

Hardcovers
Softcovers
All Ebook Formats
Audiobooks
Podcasts
Worldwide Distribution

Indie Author Services
Book Development, Editing, Proofing
Graphic/Cover Design
Video/Trailer Production
Website Creation
Social Media Marketing
Writing Contests
Writers' Blogs

Authors
Editors
Artists
Experts
Professionals

FreshInkGroup.com
info@FreshInkGroup.com
Twitter: @FreshInkGroup
Facebook.com/FreshInkGroup
LinkedIn: Fresh Ink Group

Elena Dkany inherits her family's castle in Romania, a land dipped in myths, folklore, and the legendary walking dead. The local proverb serves as warning: "Do not speak badly of the Devil, because you cannot know to whom you will belong." When she's attacked by an international assassin, only her deceased husband and her ex-boyfriend's live presence can protect her on her journey to the mountainous region of Transylvania.

But that's not the only problem troubling Elena. Who is that boy invading her dreams? And what really happened to a priceless gem-crusted silver cross buried by an earthquake in the fifteenth century? Who's stalking Elena? Who wants her dead and why?

Hardcover, Softcover, Ebooks

If you ever find yourself on the Strange Hwy—don't turn around. Don't panic. Just. Keep. Going. You never know what you'll find.

You'll see magic at the fingertips of an autistic young man; a teen girl's afternoon, lifetime of loss; a winged man, an angel? Demon—? Mother's recognition, peace to daughter; Danny's death, stifled secrets; black man's music, guitar transforms boy; dead brother, open confession; first love, supernatural? —family becomes whole!

You can exit the Strange Hwy, and come back any time you want.

See, now you know the way in, don't be a stranger.